I0739102

The Grove of Hollow Trees

The Grove of Hollow Trees

Ron McAdow

PHP
Personal History Press
Lincoln, Massachusetts

Copyright 2020 Ron McAdow
ISBN-978-0-9983619-5-6 hard cover
ISBN: 978-0-9983619-7-0 paper cover
ISBN: 978-0-9983619-9-4 e-book
Library of Congress Control Number: 2020935773

PHP

Personal History Press
Lincoln, Massachusetts

To my friends

We can with difficulty comprehend the character of a cosmic mind whose purposes are revealed by the strange mixture of goods and evils that we find in this actual world's particulars. Or rather we cannot by any possibility comprehend it.

–William James

1

"What do you want to accomplish here?"

"I'm looking for insight," Phil said.

"Too vague," the therapist said. "That's what James considered self-indulgent."

"Jim thought I was self-indulgent?"

"His notes leave that impression. We need a goal."

"A goal? Because you have a form you have to fill out?"

"Time is a limited resource. We should focus."

"I worry about my son," Phil said, "but forget that. It upsets me to hear that Jim—I really loved Jim—said that about me."

"Are you thin-skinned? I assumed that fellow professionals could be frank."

"Without sensitivity I would be a poor therapist."

"On that point there is more than one school of thought."

"What do you want me to call you?"

"Call me by my name."

"Andrew Vogelsong?"

"What did you call Dr. Freeman?"

"Jim."

"Then call me Andrew. Is your therapeutic goal to reduce your anxiety about your son?"

"Right now I am missing my gentle former therapist and his replacement says he resented me."

"I didn't say he resented you."

"Of course you did. My son—I picture him blue and frozen on the side of Mount Katahdin."

"Could that happen? Or are you expressing a fantasy?"

"It hasn't happened yet. But in my mind's eye, there he lies, where he gave himself to hypothermia."

"Is he depressed?"

"Probably. I don't know. All considered, maybe he does okay. Here's my main issue: I was born needing to know what it means to be a person."

"Wasn't everyone?"

"In my experience, no. Few trouble themselves much about it."

"Many refer that to their religious faiths."

"Not I."

"You are not a believer?"

"My family went to church and my parents sent me to Sunday school, where I learned about God's book and his oddly-begotten son. It was all of great interest to me at the time."

"You bought it."

"The adult world framed it as the Truth. The Word. The approved understanding of what life was all about."

"What church did you attend?"

"We were Presbyterian. When I was little, I disliked the scratchy outfit I had to wear to Sunday School and couldn't wait to get home and change into my play clothes. But middle-sized me looked for knowledge. My parents talked about World War II and Hitler and death camps. I feared atomic bombs and car crashes. Evil and fear of evil. Hard to make sense of, to feel okay in, yet the people around me didn't care. When I got to college I found others who thought about things and I married one of them."

"You are married?"

"No—Elaine and I are divorced."

"Have you re-married?"

"No. I have a girlfriend. My wife and I still sleep together. Once in a while. We both have other lovers—most of hers are women. Sometimes I cook for Elaine and we tell each other what we're reading. Occasionally we are intimate, although she has never been cuddly. We compare notes about Paul. Our son."

"Your girlfriend doesn't mind you consorting with your ex?"

"Lydia is married to a nice guy neither of us wants to see hurt. They have their own kids. We are polyamorous."

"Is she your patient?"

"No. I prefer to call them clients. Lydia was a client but I referred her as soon as our feelings became enmeshed. She is so great. I think about her all the time. Meanwhile, I've never stopped loving my other lovers, and I correspond with some of them. Being co-parent with Elaine puts her in a different category—although Elaine mothers to her own drummer."

"What?"

"Elaine is not maternal. She never worries about Paul."

"We have returned to your therapeutic goal: your anxieties about your son."

"My insurance will pay you without reference to some artificial objective."

"Our work together needs direction. I'm not here to follow you around some existential desert."

"When I hear you say that, I think, 'How obnoxious.'"

"I'm a professional pain in the ass," Vogelsong said.

"You are good at it," Phil said. "My son is an environmentalist. And a naturalist. Right now he is all about bears. Bears and Indians. Native Americans. In Maine. He and his friends are trying to get the Penobscot compensated for the pine trees we stole. Or something like that. He leads trips. Canoe trips. Backpacking trips. A woman helps him. They were born at my commune."

"You had a commune?"

"Yes. My friend and I went back to the earth. Briefly, in my case."

"What happened to your marriage?"

"We were too young to get married. We thought we were smart—but that was dumb. And then along came baby Paul. Skipping birth control was part of going back to nature. Followed by natural childbirth."

"You were hippies?"

"You could say so. I wouldn't use that term. We were kids with longish hair. We had a house where people lived who weren't related to us. Some drugs got done. Some premarital sex got enjoyed. A lot of music got listened to. We liked to work and to learn. Drugs were not our main thing. I was married and became a father."

"Later you divorced."

"Yes."

"Why?"

"We married too young."

"That's not inherently a cause for separation."

"Elaine is a willful person who determines precisely the distance she will keep between herself and each other person. Emotionally. I became aware of that watching her with Paul. Even with her tender-hearted warmly responsive only son she maintained a separation— less than arm's length but farther than he wanted. Seeing that, I realized that she did the same with me. I faulted her for the way she was with our son and I disliked the way she was with me and I asked for counseling and change. Her response was to move in with her girlfriend and that was that."

"Your son is depressed because he was abandoned by his mother?"

"She never truly abandoned him and I am not certain that he is depressed. One thing I should mention is that my feelings about my son are affected by a client's deep grief."

"How so?"

"He lost his children. His daughter died skiing and his son committed suicide a year to the day after his sister's death. How do you face life after that?"

"People do."

"Indeed. My client does. Somehow. Not because of any help I give him. He's one of our local geniuses and he keeps coming back these many years so I guess somehow talking with me is worth his time. He was my best friend's brother's mentor—which is how he found me to begin with. For decades I've ached for him."

"Case in point about tender-hearted therapists. Back to Sunday School. What happened with you and religion?"

"At first I believed the whole story about God and Jesus. I was earnest and idealistic. I prayed for peace and justice. When the Vietnam War got going, I asked God to stop it. But it only got worse. And racists kept on hating. I listened for answers to my prayers, but all I heard was silence. Then I began to want sex. Religion was negative about everything to do with that. I didn't give up easily. I looked for sacred texts in poems and songs and cartoons. I gave a classroom presentation about radical theologians. When I asked my teacher what he thought about my paper, he made a dismissive gesture and said, 'Phil, to me, it's all just dancing around the totem pole.'

"I thought, *Oh, It's all just dancing around the totem pole.* That explained my unanswered prayers, the violence and chaos in the world, why the Holocaust could happen. Through that lens, the chaotic world made a lot more sense. That dismissive gesture became my own mental habit. The religious behaviors and thoughts of my fellow human beings became a behavior to be observed and, if possible, understood.

"Looking back, my teacher's remark was just the last straw. It could have been anything; I was done with churches. But I still wanted to understand the big picture. I became aware of the sciences of mind and society. My search went down that road."

"You became a therapist."

"Yes."

"And you lived on a commune."

"Yes. The farm was before I became a therapist. Elaine has dough and she bought the place for me and Jeff. She was there, too, of course—but the vision was Jeff's and mine, the back-to-the-earth thing. North Road Farm, in the shadow of the Berkshires. People came. It was great."

"Yeah. So you've been roaming your existential wilderness for a long time," Vogelsong said. "When you come back, I'll want to know how I can help you."

Walking to the parking lot, Phil wondered how long he would stick with this replacement therapist. Could it be helpful, after so many years with Jim, to talk with a less congenial guy? Then he realized he had no idea where, in the acre of automobiles, he would find his car. He began to search, resolving for the thousandth time to make a mental note of where he parked.

Being grows under all sorts of resistances in this world of man, and, from compromise to compromise.
–William James

2

Karen Morelli's parents had expected her to go to college. When college turned out to be boring, Karen dropped out, took a bus to San Francisco, and became a flower child. A year later, Boomer, Karen's high school boyfriend, returned from Vietnam, bought a motorcycle, and followed Karen to Haight-Ashbury. Boomer's arrival caused Karen to re-evaluate the people she was living with. The phrase *pseudo-intellectual* popped into her mind and sped her to a decision. With Boomer's bike between her legs she watched four thousand North American miles go by.

A few months later, Karen developed appendicitis. Boomer dropped her at her parents' house in Massachusetts and rode away.

After she'd recovered from surgery, Karen gave college another try. She became a fixture on the street scene in Amherst. When Boomer showed up, got a job, and rented an apartment, she moved in with him. Her parents cut off her financial support, which meant that the next time Boomer went on the road, Karen couldn't pay her rent. When someone told her about a commune over in Dutton she decided to check it out.

At the farm, Karen talked to Phil and Elaine. "We're committed to equality," Phil told her.

"Equality's good," Karen agreed.

Staring from beneath dark bangs, Elaine asked Karen if she had read *The Golden Notebook* or Betty Friedan.

"I've heard of them," Karen replied. "I'm not that much of a reader. But I'm a good cook."

"We're vegetarian," Elaine said.

"That's okay," Karen said, but inwardly she recoiled.

When Phil asked, "Are you a farmer?" Karen said she'd think about it.

Back in Amherst, friends invited Karen to take LSD. In the middle of the ensuing three-day psychedelic experience, she returned to her apartment and put her key in the door. It wouldn't turn. *Kare's locked out!* became the refrain of the drug trip. It wasn't as funny to Karen as it was to the others.

When the LSD wore off Karen went to the landlord, who had changed the lock. He handed her a black plastic trash bag containing her clothes, and wished her luck.

Karen hitchhiked to the farmhouse in Dutton. As she approached the front door a young man came onto the porch. He had long brown hair and a handsome face. He was smoking a hand-rolled cigarette, which Karen correctly assumed contained marijuana. "Guess what?" she called out, in her too-loud voice. "I'm a farmer!"

"Want a hit?" the man asked. His name was Jeff Quarless.

Karen deposited her trash bag onto the porch, lowered herself into an old wooden chair, and accepted the joint.

Boomer showed up a week later. He helped fix the farm's tractor and gave unsolicited advice about home maintenance. Boomer came and went, but Karen stuck around. In mid-February Boomer had been gone for a month and Karen didn't know when or whether he would return.

Except for Halloween, holidays meant little at the farm, but Jeff had always liked Valentine's Day. The afternoon of February fourteenth he baked a tray of brownies and carved brownie hearts for each of the women. Elaine wasn't there, so he left hers on the table. When he handed one to Karen, she said, "For later, when I'm stoned," and gave him an inviting look.

After Jeff finished washing the dinner dishes he went to Karen's room, which was furnished with a beat-up dresser and a mattress on the floor. Karen turned out the light, lit a candle, and closed the curtains she had made from burlap feed sacks.

Jeff sat on the edge of her mattress—there was no chair. Karen took a metal box from the top drawer of her dresser. It was red with an Indian design printed on the top. She handed it, and a packet of rolling papers, to Jeff. "Will you?"

"Surely, ma'am." Jeff opened the box and smelled the marijuana. He took a paper from the packet and held it in his left hand while he sprinkled the dried leaf-flakes into it with the fingers of his right.

Karen sat down beside him. "I wish my stereo hadn't gotten stolen."

"When did that happen?"

"In San Francisco. Bastards."

"Bummer."

"Yeah. Oh well." Karen watched him complete the joint by twisting one end. Then he struck a match. In the light of the candle and the match, Jeff looked nice. He was nice. He took a first quick toke to get the marijuana glowing and passed the joint to Karen. "Thank you, boss man," she said. This was rebellious on Karen's part, because the group preferred to think it had no boss. Phil facilitated their morning meetings and functioned as administrator—but Jeff had more charisma and practical know-how. Rubble, the strapping kid, deferred to him, which gave Jeff, in Karen's eyes, a high status that was part of his attractiveness. She filled her lungs with smoke, paused, then slowly exhaled.

"Pretty good stuff," Jeff said.

They both knew how to get stoned. When the joint was gone, Karen offered Jeff a back rub. In answer, he stretched out on her mattress. Karen massaged his back and shoulders for five minutes, then said, "My turn."

Jeff began with her shoulders, descended her spine, skipped down to her knees and calves, lingered on her feet, then he started back up her legs. This time he did not cheat her middle region. After a minute of being stimulated through her jeans, Karen rolled over and took them off.

Jeff undressed. Karen's bedding was sleeping bags that she had bought for camping with a boyfriend in California. When Jeff was above her, Karen pulled the edge of a bag over his shoulders, put her arms around him, and sighed happily.

Twenty minutes later, Jeff's mind became un-sexed. What would his pleasure cost him? By going to bed with Karen, had he promised a relationship? If Boomer returned, would there be trouble?

"Want another joint?" Karen asked.

Jeff rolled off onto his side. "No. That was great. I'm not sure it was a good idea, but it was great."

"Yeah."

Thank you, Jeff almost said, but he caught himself. He rolled out from under the sleeping bag and found his clothes.

Karen sat up and lit a tobacco cigarette. She wondered, briefly, why she didn't feel guilty about cheating on Boomer. She remembered the brownie and its pink frosting and looked forward to eating it.

Jeff went downstairs.

Phil and Elaine were at the kitchen table. Elaine's brownie was in front of her. When Jeff came in, she looked up. "What the hell is this?"

"It's your valentine."

"What's that supposed to mean?"

"It's supposed to be friendly. You sound offended."

"It worries me."

"Why worry? Didn't you get valentines in school?"

"Sure." Elaine jerked her thumb toward her husband. "Where's Phil's?"

"I didn't make one for Phil."

"In school we gave one to everybody."

"Phil can have the trimmings."

"Jeff, what's this valentines crap really about, anyway?"

"It's just a brownie."

"Bullshit. You carved it into a heart. Are you giving me your heart? Shall we fall in love?"

"Jesus, Elaine."

"It is not just a brownie. Maybe that's all you meant by it, okay, but people have to start thinking about stuff. Because these things are part of the paternalistic system, whether you know it or not."

"I have to get my consciousness raised?"

"If the shoe fits, wear it."

"This late at night, clichés are okay?"

"Fuck you."

Jeff looked at Phil. "Could you see this coming?"

Phil asked Elaine whether she might be overreacting because wasn't it basically a good thing to receive a brownie?

"Maybe. Maybe I am overreacting. Maybe it's just my hormones, right? I'm too emotional, right? Or maybe the guys around here just can't or don't want to step back and look at reality."

"We all want a better world," Phil said. "Do we have to throw out every tradition?"

"We have to think about our actions and what they communicate and not just act like lemmings as though everything our second grade teachers told us to do was right."

Neither man spoke.

"Okay, guys. Okay, Jeff." Leaving her brownie on the table, Elaine stood up. "Thanks for the valentine. I'm going to bed. We can discuss this at the meeting."

Jeff thought, *There's something to look forward to.*

"Sorry, man," Phil said, when Elaine was out of earshot. "We can talk it through."

"I made it with Karen tonight."

"You did?"

"Yeah. We had a joint and . . . "

"Okay. Wow."

"Valentine's Day put her in the mood, I guess, and the joint put me in the mood. Crap. I was just trying to be nice."

Phil shrugged. "Love the one you're with . . . "

"Maybe I fucked up?"

"We're just living our life, man. Like we said we would."

Jeff looked at the bench he was sitting on. He had built it and painted it with dark green enamel—the color he thought benches should be.

Phil rinsed the tea cups. As he started up the stairs, he gave Jeff a wry look. "Goodnight, man. Happy Valentine's Day."

Jeff wanted to talk with his brother, who was in business school in Boston. The long-distance rates were low at this time of night, in-state, but the farm's one phone offered no privacy. Jeff decided to write him a letter. He went to his room, where a wooden chest he had made in high school shop class held his non-communal possessions, including his writing materials. Back at the kitchen table, he began, *Dear Bob, Have you started making money yet? Millions? Did you do anything about Valentine's Day? Watch out!*

Thinking and acting are just two names for a single process—the process of making our way as best we can in a universe shot through with contingency.

–Louis Menand

3

Get your metabolism going early, so your body will burn
more calories. Because Bob had adopted this advice he pedaled his
stationary bike in his pajamas, four minutes, as the coffee brewed. Bob
was sixty-four years old and he liked to eat and drink. His doctor's
height-weight table disapproved of the result. Bob felt good and
he thought he looked okay but he was supposed to be lighter. He
believed he was about to have a lot more time to exercise. He had
found a buyer for his company and the closing was today. Tomorrow
would be the first day of a new era. For the rest of his life, he told
himself, his time would be his own.

Bob's law firm was in Boston, in the financial district, in a
glass-sheathed office building. The adjacent parking garage was a
destination in the navigation system of Bob's Lexus. He used it, not
because he didn't know the way, but because its prompts would call
him back if his thoughts wandered. He liked his thoughts to wander
but he did not, this morning, want to miss a turn and have to guess
his way through Boston's maze of crooked streets.

Bob left his car in the garage and stepped into an elevator.
His shoulder bag was almost empty — it contained his small laptop
computer and his business cards. His lawyers had the documents.
Bob was founder and chief executive of Thundercloud Systems; all he
needed today, to close the sale, was his signature.

An attorney named Jay Phelps walked Bob to a conference room.
When the door closed behind them Jay said, "Bob, have you talked
to Peter today?" Peter was CEO of the corporation poised to trade its
stock for Thundercloud Systems.

"No. Why?" Bob wished that his brain would not remind him
that Jay, a slender, clean-shaven man of forty, was gay. Bob was
thoroughly at home in liberal Massachusetts; he suffered private

embarrassment that some part of him bothered to remember that Jay was homosexual.

"They lost value yesterday," Jay said. The amount of stock that Bob and his investors would receive was pegged to the market price.

"Yeah, I saw that, but they are still in their range." Bob was aware that if the purchaser's shares went too low the deal was off.

"They're down nearly to the threshold. That's okay with Peter but he's got board members who are unhappy. One guy thinks the range is too big, that it goes too low, and he's pressuring Peter to delay or renegotiate."

"Fuck."

"As you say. But Peter's working the problem. He wants to go ahead. So stay tuned."

Jay left Bob in the conference room. The glass wall gave an ocean view. The horizon was far out over the Atlantic. Bob wondered, how far, from this height? The foreground was the financial district. Between the office buildings and the ocean lay a fleet of little islands at anchor in the blue of Boston Harbor. Bob drained the landscape, in his imagination, and pictured mastodons grazing between the ice-age hills whose tops, when the ice sheet melted, had become the islands.

Bob's phone chimed—a text had arrived. It was from his brother. *Good luck today.*

Rocky start, Bob replied. He pictured Jeff's calm face and resolved, for the thousandth time, to be more like him.

Jeff responded, *Hang tough.*

Will do.

Through the clear air Bob watched a boat leave Boston Harbor. He called Peter, and Peter answered. For months of negotiations they had used each other's cell numbers for texts and for occasional conversations.

"Hey Bob."

"Peter. Jay says you've got some headaches."

"Yeah. I might need to buy a little time."

Bob wondered what provision of the sale contract Peter thought gave him wiggle room on timing. "Today's a good day to close." Bob played on the warrior's laconic pledge *it's a good day to die* without knowing whether Peter would follow the reference.

"Right. I agree. If possible, we shall."

"We made a clear understanding."

"Give me a couple of hours."

"Okay. See you later." Making that call was all Bob could do about his problem. He sank into a remarkably comfortable leather-covered chair. This high above the street the scene through the window was static. It was all background. Boats were few, small, and distant; the view was buildings, sky, and sea. Bob wondered how he would actually spend his retirement. Building boats in his shop? He loved to work with wood but maybe he should find some new way to express himself, like painting. Should he take watercolor lessons? Or maybe he could compose music. He felt that he had creative potential—but he wasn't sure what kind of creative potential.

Why hadn't he developed an artistic self at an earlier point in his life? He had pursued multiple goals. He had wanted to get married, to raise children, and to be of service to his town and to the world in general. And also to be in some way creative—although he considered that goal more narcissistic than the others. He had reasoned when he was in college that if he started a company he would create jobs, which, he predicted, would be more helpful to society than anything his do-gooder college friends were likely to achieve through political campaigns or their various "movements" for uplifting the downtrodden. Plus, a business would spin off income to support a family, would generate life experience, and, in the end, if he succeeded, make him rich enough to spend his time however he liked.

Bob had not expected it to take this many years to reach that outcome, although when he reviewed the phases of his career he thought he ought to have foreseen the probability. First, in his early twenties, he'd gone to business school, followed by a few years of employment in the software industry to make contacts and to identify a promising area of the emerging digital technology. That was in the nineteen seventies, when many educated persons sniffed at business and regarded businessmen as a drag on progress—a regressive social force—which had put Bob under suspicion of being a traitor to his generation.

Meanwhile, he had married Ruth. Their son was still in pre-school when Bob had become a junior-level founder of his first startup, which had eventually been sold. Bob had made money but not big money. After a few years of consulting he had co-founded a second company. Its chief executive officer was his best friend, who died in a mountaineering accident just before they were scheduled to go public. Shaken by his friend's death, Bob sold his equity. He used the money for his son's education—with enough left over to be a major investor in this third startup. The new millennium had arrived, and by the time Bob and his team were ready to reap a big reward for having started Thundercloud Systems, the Great Recession brought everything to a halt.

With the recession over, Bob believed that he finally had his independence teed up.

The conference room door opened. Jay stepped in and said, "It's not looking good." At the same time a text arrived on Bob's phone. It was from Peter. *Not today sorry soon I hope.*

Because his wife had worked the previous night Bob knew she would be trying to sleep. When he got home he peeked into their bedroom.

"How did it go?" Ruth asked.

"It went poorly."

"Damn. I'm getting up. Want some coffee?"

"I want a beer. How was your night?"

"On a scale of one to ten, five. What went wrong with your thing?"

"Peter's company's stock lost value last week. So they'd have to make up the difference with more shares and Peter has a guy on his board who thinks that's a bad idea."

"Can't you take less stock and get it done?"

"I cannot." Bob, himself, would have been willing to renegotiate, but he knew that his board was in no hurry to sell and that they would insist on the agreed-upon value.

"What do you do now?"

"Wait. See how their stock moves this week."

"Ugh."

"Yes."

"Sorry."

"Perseverance furthers."

This line from the *I Ching* had been a byword between Bob and Ruth during their child-raising years—their son had been a challenge. As soon as he had entered kindergarten, Ruth had gone to medical school. She was now supervisor of emergency services department at a Boston hospital.

Ruth looked around the kitchen. There were dirty dishes on the counter. "I thought you were going to empty the dishwasher."

"Sorry."

"What are you going to do now?"

"Empty the dishwasher."

"After that?"

"Re-fill it."

"After that?"

"The treadmill."

"I'll make supper."

"Thanks. Jeff texted me. He wished me luck."

"What for?"

"My closing. He remembered it was today."

"It didn't work."

"He's a good guy."

"Yeah. Different subject, but related: Annie and Jack want to go out to dinner with us."

"Tonight?"

"No, they are still in Belize. On Saturday. Okay?"

"Sure."

"Want some chèvre?"

Life is trouble. Only death is not. To be alive is to undo your belt and look for trouble."

–Nikos Kazantzakis, Zorba the Greek

4

The morning after he had sex with Karen, Jeff got up early. He decided to work in the barn, where it was cold and quiet and he could think. The workbench in the barn's shop was cluttered with nuts and bolts and screws accumulated by previous farmers. The task of sorting them was too big and too boring for sustained attention; Jeff did it a little at a time. He turned on the light over the work bench, savored the cold-barn smell, removed one mitten, and started dropping wood screws into coffee cans. *Clink.* Might Karen and he become a couple? *Clink.* Did he want that? *Clink.* He liked Karen as a person. Had the intimacy generated emotion? Protectiveness, maybe. Romance, no. He didn't want to hurt her feelings. Was he jealous of her past with Boomer? Did that turn him off? Did fear of Boomer keep him from seeking the role of boyfriend? What would happen when Boomer turned up?

"That was nice, last night," Karen said.

Startled, Jeff looked over his shoulder. There she was, in the doorway, hugging herself to keep warm. "Yeah, it was great."

"Are we happening?"

"I don't know."

"I guess we're not."

"I have to think."

"You are great."

"So are you."

"Why do you have to think?"

"I might not be ready."

"To be a man for a woman?"

Jeff looked at a can marked "WOOD SCREWS MEDIUM."

"You're afraid of Boomer."

"Right."

"Sorry. I know you aren't."

Jeff looked back at her.

"I could help you make this place happen," she promised.

"Yeah."

"Unless I had to be friends with Elaine."

"You have a problem with Elaine?"

"She has a problem with me and I have a problem with that."

"She should get over it. As for us, I'm not sure yet. Maybe I shouldn't have come up last night."

"Okay. Well, damn. Let me know if you figure it out."

Through the dirty barn window Jeff watched Karen walk back to the house. From behind, she looked a little bulky. Jeff wasn't drawn to her. *We shouldn't have made it,* he thought. After he dropped ten more screws into cans, he decided to go to town. He turned off the shop's light and went out to the communal truck, an aged red Ford pickup, parked beside the house. The keys were always in the ignition. Jeff pulled out the choke, then turned the key. The engine rumbled, then fired and started. Leaving the truck to warm up, Jeff went into the house.

Elaine was at the kitchen table. "Headed out?"

"Yup."

"I was not nice last night. About the valentine."

"That's okay."

"It's just all that old romantic stuff turns out to be bad for women. You know? But you are as liberated as any guy, I get that, and you meant well. It's how we were brought up; it sneaks up on us."

"It's okay. Won't happen again. Need anything not on the list?"

"Nah. Bye."

"See you."

At the café in the town's center, Jeff picked up a newspaper and sat down at the counter. The waitress brought him coffee, called him "dear," and took his order. He skimmed the paper. The school budget didn't concern him. Neither did most of the other local news—it illustrated the gap between the town's consciousness and that of Jeff and his friends. The town chugged along as if there had been no cultural upheaval—as if the Vietnam War and the sexual revolution and the civil rights movement had never happened. Whatever occurred elsewhere, here in New England the town and church committees and school calendars proceeded as they had for centuries.

Jeff worked his way through the paper as he ate breakfast. When the waitress removed his plate he started on the classified advertising. *Maybe I should get a job,* he thought. He had already discussed this possibility with Phil, who hoped he would not. "Plenty to do around here, man," Phil had said, referring to improvements to the house and barn that had kept Jeff busy for the first eight months at the farm.

"Yeah but we need cash, too," Jeff had responded. "We have to buy stuff. My savings won't last forever." Elaine's money, on the other hand, would last forever, but to preserve the equality of their partnership Phil and he pretended to disregard her wealth.

Jeff used the cafe's pay phone to call about an item he found under Help Wanted. A secretary invited Jeff to drive up and fill out an application, which he did. After a short interview, a manager said they'd let him know. When he got back to the farm he told Phil, "I applied for a job."

"Part-time?"

"No. They need full time."

"Where?"

"Greylock Music Center. Maintenance."

"How would you get there?"

"Dunno. I'd need a ride. I guess I'd buy some wheels."

"So that's it for the farm, huh?"

"No, man. It just means I won't be broke. If I get the job I can help pay the bills."

"You'd be gone all day."

"I can still get stuff done here."

"You'd miss morning meeting."

"Bummer."

"We could make money with this farm, you know. Selling eggs and produce and stuff. Asparagus."

"We won't have asparagus to sell for two or three years. And it costs more to feed the chickens than we can get for eggs."

"I don't know, man. It sounds like a slippery slope."

"I probably won't get it anyway."

Two days later Greylock Music Center's head of maintenance called and offered Jeff the job. He accepted. That night at supper he announced his news and asked if anyone would take him to work. "I'll get a car as soon as I can."

"Why do you want a job?" Karen asked.

"I can use the bread. We can use the bread."

"Good luck, man," Phil said.

"I'll take you," Karen said.

Jeff's first day of work was the following Monday. Karen was late coming down. Because he was determined to be on time, to avoid confirming anyone's assumption that long-haired young men were irresponsible, Jeff had allowed for the probability of Karen's tardiness. When she emerged from the house and climbed into the truck the engine and the cab were already warm. When Jeff turned the truck onto the road Karen asked, "What will you do at this place?"

"Whatever needs doing, I guess. Buildings and grounds. Helping out."

"What kind of music do they have there?"

"Classical. Orchestras play there in the summer."

"Why are they hiring you in the middle of winter?"

"They have maintenance work all year."

"Are you okay about us?"

"Yeah. You are so fine but—"

"We aren't a thing."

"I don't know."

"If we were, you'd know."

"Maybe. I don't know."

"Boomer will show up someday."

"Yeah."

"No sweat for you?"

"No sweat."

O to be self-balanced for contingencies,
to confront night, storms, hunger, ridicule, accidents, rebuffs,
as the trees and animals do.
–Walt Whitman

5

Jen awakened worried that Jack would embarrass her again.

She poked her travel clock, which lit to show she had ten more minutes before the alarm went off. Her unconscious brain had been minding the time. She inhaled warm air and tried to relax. *Don't let him get under your skin,* she told herself. *Trust Paul. Chill. Aguacaliente.* She loved that sound—the name of their location in Belize, and also of this eco-lodge.

Turning on her bedside lamp, Jen surveyed the floor of her cabana. She did not want to put a foot down on a spider or centipede or scorpion or any other creepy-crawly. *This isn't the desert,* she reminded herself. *No scorpions.* "Aguacaliente," she said out loud.

She thought again of the man who had seemed to take pleasure in making her feel unprepared. Should she have learned all about the Mayans? She had worked hard to be ready on the natural history of the region. Birds were the main focus for most participants. Jen knew what species were to be looked for where, and she had memorized their calls. This was her second trip to Belize with Paul Scribner. Officially, she was co-leader but really she was Paul's helper. She wanted to do well, to avoid disappointing her friend, and because the job of shepherding eco-tourists on nature-centric travel gave her a chance to see places she otherwise couldn't afford to visit.

Jen's pre-trip study had not been limited to birds. She had made herself knowledgeable about as many aspects of Central American nature as she could. She had spent time on butterflies, and on spiders, attempting to overcome her visceral revulsion. She had learned the most common trees and shrubs and had reviewed ferns and orchids. She had decided not to attempt expertise at Mayan ruins because they would always be working with local guides and she agreed with Paul that it was best to give them a monopoly on interpreting local culture.

Howler monkeys called Jen back to the moment. She tried to shake off her defensive mind-set. She thought about the day ahead, what to wear, reminded herself to email her mom, wondered what she should say, and felt the familiar disappointment about her mother's limitations. Jen stepped out the door and let the fresh air and the exuberant plant life re-center her.

When she reached the dining common Jen poured herself some coffee and sat down with Paul and Ruben, who were conferring about the day ahead. She tried to focus on what they were saying but her attention caught on Paul's facial hair—his bushy beard and mouth-covering mustache. She wondered how Laura could stand kissing him—it would be so ticklish and furry. I could ask Laura, she thought, but she knew she never would. She and Laura were polite to each other but they were both private and never discussed personal topics. Jen suspected that Laura was jealous of her long friendship with Paul. She shifted her gaze to Ruben. His brown cheeks were smooth and his eyes looked happier than Paul's.

"Have they got both manakins?" Paul asked.

"No," Ruben replied. "Most of them have the white-collared. But we did not see red-capped yesterday."

"The repeaters probably have them from other trips," Paul said. "Still, while we're looking for antbirds let's not forget about manakins." Hearing himself say the funny-sounding bird names made Paul grin, which Jen thought changed his look from sad to wise.

Paul *was* wise, Jen thought. She associated the phrase *old soul* with this man. Sometimes people called her an old soul, too, but she disagreed because she thought an old soul carried the consciousness of many generations of humanity. The burden grounded you and gave you a certain solemn contentment. Jen did not feel grounded and had only intervals of contentment.

"Jen, do you want your own group today?" Paul asked.

"Sure," she replied, because she thought that was what he expected of her. She considered adding the condition that Jack Bigelow not be in her group, but pride kept her from it.

When everyone had emerged from the vans for the first of the day's walks, Paul announced the groups and assigned them to leaders. Jack Bigelow and Annie Brown and another couple named Anderson-Barr were to be with Jen. She braced herself.

The vehicles were parked at the middle of two trail loops that made a figure eight. Each of the groups was to take separate routes. Jen and her foursome began a clockwise circuit of the north loop. Right away Jen started spotting birds. As soon as she saw one she tried to help the others locate the dot of color in the foliage before the bird disappeared. Giving clear, effective directions was the biggest challenge of being a bird guide. When Jen succeeded at this she felt lucky; when she failed she felt incompetent.

Following Jen's clues, Jack saw the bird. "A tanager. Which?"

"Crimson-collared."

Jen kept finding birds. Half an hour later, when her group met Ruben's, they had already seen twenty species. Ruben had only twelve but these included scarlet macaws. Jen hurried her group forward, hoping the showy red birds might still be near the trail. They were—everyone had a good look.

"What's that?" Jack asked, pointing toward a bird to their right.

When she had it in her binoculars, Jen gasped. "It's a lovely cotinga. A new species for me!"

Annie's face seemed stuck to her camera. Its shutter clicked again and again.

Looking at another small bird, Jack said, "If that's a honeycreeper it would be my first."

"That's it!" Jen said. "Green honeycreeper."

The colorful little bird turned to show its back, then flew into bright light as if to pose for a photograph.

That was how the morning went. Birding fortune favored Jen and her group. They saw so many more species than the others that Jen was embarrassed to hear Jack Bigelow report their count to Paul and Ruben— because her confirming nod felt like a boast.

Back at the lodge, at lunch, the five of them sat apart from the others to coordinate their checklists, which extended the existence of their group and allowed them to enjoy, for a few minutes more, their sense of shared good fortune.

When the Anderson-Barrs rose to go to their cabana, Annie went with them but Jack stayed at the table. As soon as they were alone he said, "Thanks for the morning."

"I'm glad you enjoyed it. I did, too."

"I had a great time."

"We had an unusual number of what Paul calls Q.E.s."

"Q.E.s?"

"Quality encounters," Jen explained. "Like with the honeycreeper, when he gave us such a great look."

"Ah. Term of art."

"Yes. In the eco-tour guide biz. Really it's just Paul-speak. Maybe it will catch on."

"You guys are good," Jack said. He played with his napkin, rolling and folding it. "Did it seem like I gave you a hard time yesterday?"

"I could see why you would expect—"

"Annie thought you might have taken me the wrong way."

Jen looked at him. "It sounded like you were disappointed that . . . but I shouldn't be so sensitive. I just don't want to disappoint anyone."

"You didn't. I shouldn't have teased you."

"We have the theory that we ought to let the local guides do the Mayan stuff."

"Makes sense. Sorry."

Jen relaxed.

"How do you happen to work with Ruben?" Jack asked.

"Paul met Ruben years ago, here at Aguacaliente. He has a lot of respect for Ruben and always arranges to work with him when he brings people here."

"Meanwhile you and Paul seem well matched—and you have plenty of history." Jack raised his eyebrows to communicate a question.

"No!" Jen answered. "He lives with his girlfriend."

"Is that so?"

"Yeah. So we're kind of brother and sister. He was actually physically born at the farm, I think. Maybe you know more about it than I do." Although she had never met them before the trip, Jen was aware that Jack and Annie had lived at North Road Farm, in the early seventies, with her mother.

"I remember it well," Jack said. "Elaine delivered Paul on the kitchen table. Annie took pictures. And your mom became pregnant with you, but she left, we all left, before you were born."

"Why were you there? Did you like it?"

"We were graduate students and Annie was writing her dissertation and I was supposedly figuring out the topic of mine."

"Did you both get PhD s?"

"Eventually. But all I did at the farm was work on my dome and think of myself as a sort of Anglo-Native American. And get high."

"You built the dome?"

"It's still standing?"

"Yeah. I think Jeff goes in there to smoke."

Jack laughed. "That's appropriate. Do you hear much about those years?"

"A little. Mom mentions stuff sometimes."

"Annie tells me there's going to be a reunion in a few weeks." Jack stood up. "Thanks again for the birds," he said, and he walked away.

That evening, when Jen got around to doing email, she considered how easy it was to lose her mother's attention and abandoned the idea of writing a long message. *She'll just want to know I'm okay*, Jen thought. She wrote, *Mom, I got your message yesterday. I'm in Belize, you know, guiding with Paul. We fly home tomorrow. Yes, I'll come and help on Saturday.*

It was Jen's last night at Aguacaliente. She closed her computer, went to the porch, and sat in the dark. Wherever it touched her skin the mild moist air soothed and reassured her. She inhaled with deep pleasure until she detected an odor of burning trash from a nearby village. A mosquito stabbed her bare arm. As she slapped she noticed a headlamp coming down the trail. She heard a man's voice. Instead of continuing past her cabana the lamp turned toward Jen. Paul said, "Hello Jen. Jack and I were just on the subject of Baxter State Park. He's spent a lot of time up there."

"Not recently," Jack said, "but in my younger days. It's a long way from Aguacaliente."

"I've never been," Jen said. "I know Paul loves it."

"He tells me that he guides river trips," Jack said.

"It's past my bedtime," Paul said. "Goodnight, Jen. Good trip. Well done. Thanks."

"You're welcome. And thank you, I learned a lot and had a good time."

Paul walked into the dark.

"It was a good trip," Jack said. "That hike with you, when we saw so many species—that was a highlight."

"It was a lucky day."

"You are a good leader. Annie feels the same way—we think highly of you."

Jen was conscious of being alone in the dark with an interesting, articulate, man—but he was too old and too married. She wondered whether his reference to his wife was a reminder to himself—or was he so vain he thought he had to keep her from getting ideas?

"What do you go back to at home?" Jack asked.

"My job. I work in a frame shop." Jen thought, *He's asking if I have a boyfriend.* "And my mom, because this weekend she and I are selling cheese at a harvest fair." Recalling their connection with the farm, she added, "We're helping Jeff and Barb!"

"Are they still making goat cheese?"

"Yes. It's very popular."

"A harvest fair. In this climate it's hard to remember that it will be autumn in New England. Good night."

"Good night."

Jen thought, *Maybe he thinks I'm lesbian.* She wondered why she didn't have a boyfriend; why she didn't much care; why she wasn't more lonesome. Feeling chilly, she went inside and went to bed.

The harvest fair was in a college town on the Connecticut River. Jen arrived early and walked through the aisles of vendors looking for the banner with the Jeff and Barb's logo—a goat and a honeybee. When she found the North Road Farm booth, there was her mother, smoking a cigarette. "Is that allowed here?" Jen asked.

"It's okay until they open," Karen said. "How are you? What have you been up to?"

"I just got back from Belize."

"How was it?"

"It was good. Paul and Ruben were wonderful. I'm getting better."

"Bird-watching, right?"

"Yes. I have pictures. I can show you a black-faced grosbeak."

"Grosbeaks. I used to get them. It's time to set up my feeder."

"You didn't get black-faced grosbeaks. What could I do to help?"

"Nothing. Jeff and Barb came early and set everything up for us."

Jen looked at an empty space on the table. "Shouldn't we put out some samples?"

"Oh. Yeah. I suppose they want us to do that at the last minute."

As they took cheese from coolers and opened cracker boxes, Karen explained that, although she could get it cheaper at Costco, she planned to keep buying her birdseed from Ripley's Feed and Farm. "There might be changes this year. Tink and Sheila are splitting up and of course it's his family's business but she's got the brains, she's run the place forever, so will she still be there? Complicated. But what do you care? Tell me more about your trip."

It was too late. The gates opened and customers arrived. Jen and her mother gave samples, made sales, and shared in the general admiration of perfect October weather.

During a lull a little girl appeared. Her chin just reached the table-top. Her wide round eyes scanned the objects on the table, stopped on the plate of crackers, and looked up at Jen.

"Would you like a cracker?"

She nodded.

A man appeared behind the girl, but Jen kept her eyes on the child. "Would you like some cheese on your cracker?"

The girl shook her head.

"I would like to try the cheese," the man said, "and she can have my cracker."

Jen handed the girl two crackers.

"What now?" the man stage-whispered to the girl.

"Thank you," the girl said, barely audibly.

The man lowered his hand and the girl grasped two of his fingers.

"She's a cute little thing," Karen said to the man.

Jen winced.

"What's wrong with that?" Karen asked Jen. "She is."

The man tasted cheese and bought some. The girl ate both of her crackers and accepted a third. Others arrived wanting a taste of North Road Farm goat cheese, and business was steady for half an hour. During the next slow-down, Jen told her mother that she wanted to know more about her dad.

"He's been gone a long time."

"I still miss him."

"You never met him."

"I miss having a dad."

"What got you onto that? Oh. That little girl. With the man. Well. He had a good heart. Boomer had a good heart."

"His last name was Justice."

"Right."

"Why—I mean, I'm fine with it, I just wonder—why you gave me your last name instead of his."

"You can change it if you want."

"No, no, I just . . . hello Jeff and Barb," Jen said, to the man and woman who had come up behind Karen.

"Jen! What are you doing here?" Jeff asked.

"She's giving your crackers away to cute kids," Karen said.

"Give them to the ugly ones, too," Barb instructed.

"Checking up on us?" Karen asked.

"We're on our way up to Greenfield," Jeff explained. "We realized we don't have any Garlic Lovers' so we came to borrow some from you if that's okay."

"It's all yours so how much do you want?" Karen asked, as she watched her daughter locate the garlic-flavored cheese. "Too bad Jen's so free with your crackers but it's good to have her out here in public where I can show her to the guys so maybe she can find somebody."

"Mother please shut up," Jen said.

"She was just asking me about Boomer."

Jeff and Barb looked sympathetically at Jen.

"He was never a guy who was probably going to die of old age," Karen continued, "but he ought to have at least stuck around to do some daddy-ing of his kid."

Customers arrived. As Jeff described their products and made a sale, Barb suggested a change in plans. She and Karen could stay here and Jen could go on up to Greenfield with Jeff. That way one of the North Road Farmers would be at each location.

Karen and Jen were agreeable. Ten minutes later, Jen was on the passenger side of Jeff's pickup. "One of your old housemates went on a birding trip I just came back from," she said.

"Who was that?"

"Jack Bigelow. His wife went, too."

"I always liked them. Jack and Annie."

"He says he built the dome."

"He did. Are they coming to the party?"

"I think so. When is it?"

"Weekend after next. Hope you can make it."

"I might have to work."

"We'd love to have you there. You and Paul—you are our stars."

"What do you remember about my dad?" Jen hadn't planned to ask that—she hated to sound pathetic. She braced herself to be dismissed. She imagined Jeff responding that was a long time ago in a tone that reproached her neediness.

"He was a great guy. Boomer was solid. We were glad to have him in the group."

Jen drank the words.

"I'm glad you brought it up," Jeff added, "because it reminds me that I want to offer a toast to him at the get-together."

"Why was the group glad to have him?"

"Most of the rest of us were kind of in our heads. Hung-up. But Boomer was different—he was a vet; he had served in Vietnam, and he rode his bike, and the rest of us were college draft dodgers. Your dad, and your mom, too, they were earthier."

"Practical?"

"Yes and we needed that balance."

The truck was quiet as Jen thought about what it would have meant to have grown up with two parents. When she noticed the long pause, she asked, "Why do you and Barb do the cheese?" *That was random,* she thought.

Jeff replied, "For fun. For something to do with the milk. Because it tastes good. Barb loves goats and I think they're funny."

"Amazing what goes into a nanny's mouth," Jeff resumed, as they set up their booth. "Shrubbery, grass, seeds—and the goat and Barb and turn it into wonderful cheese."

"Could you make a living from cheese and honey if you wanted to?" Jen was happy to be with Jeff but she felt guilty, as though she had abandoned her mother.

"Maybe. It would be scanty. We've thought about it. But I'd miss Greylock."

Jen pictured the Greylock Music Center's grassy bowl, dotted with shade trees.

"How was your trip?" Jeff asked. "We interrupted you telling your mom about it."

"She's not that interested." Jen instantly regretted having whined.

"I've known a lot of parents like that."

"Like what?"

"Like they won't show their kids how interested they are. But they talk them up to others."

"Oh yeah?"

"Yes. With obvious pride."

Jen felt herself blush. She wondered why Barb and Jeff hadn't had any kids. "Can I come up to the farm in the morning? To see the goats?"

"Sure. We'll count on you for breakfast. Was Paul on the trip, too?"

"Yes. He's the leader. I'm his understudy."

"He's your boss?"

"Yeah."

"Is he a good boss?"

"Sure. We've always gotten along."

"I hope you can come to the party."

"I'll see. It sounds like fun."

After the Greenfield fair, Jeff dropped Jen at her mother's house. Karen was on the front porch holding a tall glass. As Jen came up the steps, her mother asked, "Want a gin and tonic?"

"Okay."

Karen didn't get up. "Sell any cheese?"

"Sold out. We also sold a little honey. But people love the cheese."

"Goat cheese. And local. Local's the big thing now."

"Seems like."

"Didn't used to be. When I was on the farm nobody cared about that."

"Why didn't you go back after you had me?"

"I was done. It was time to grow up and move on."

"Ah."

"Plus there was that bitch Elaine. Women's libber. No-balls Philip. Jeff did all the work, him and the big kid; Elaine and Phil just talked. Oh my god did they talk."

"What about?"

"Every little thing had to be gone over. And over and over. Once Boomer was gone I didn't have anybody at the farm. I always liked Jeff"—she laughed—"Who wouldn't? But Barb came and he got tight with her."

Jen pictured her young mother liking young Jeff. She herself liked old Jeff—in the sense of feeling good when she was around him. "So Jeff might have been my father?"

"What?"

"If things had been different. Because you liked him and I guess he liked you because you're still friends."

"Oh I get you. Yeah. Maybe we would have been a couple but I had Boomer and then Barb came along so we always stayed just friends, mostly, but back then I guess there was a spark. He gave me a valentine once."

"Did he?"

"Yeah, but he gave one to all the ladies."

"Oh."

"Maybe mine meant a little more. That was before Barb." Karen blew a cloud of smoke across the porch.

"I'm going to the farm in the morning," Jen said.

"What for?"

"To see the goats. Want to go with?"

"Nah. Their party's coming up."

"Jeff told me."

"They're inviting everyone who ever was at the farm. Want to go?"

"Which day?"

"All weekend. That's how the Halloween parties went. Long weekends. Halloween was big at the farm. Back in the day."

The triteness of "back in the day" caught Jen's attention. She scowled inwardly at herself for feeling superior. As for the party, did she really want to come back to Dutton and hang out with her mother's generation? "I'll think about it. What should we have for supper?"

"Want to order a pizza?"

"No. Have you been eating healthy?"

"Yes."

"I didn't see anything healthy in the fridge."

"It's in the freezer."

"Frozen entrees." Jen had noticed them and was pretty sure they had lain undisturbed since her last visit, a month before. "I'm going to the market."

"Suit yourself."

Jen returned with steaks, broccoli, and sweet potatoes. The beef was an attempt to please her mother; although she didn't consider herself a vegetarian, she usually made meals as though she were. By offering red meat, Jen hoped to avoid the thousandth repetition of her mother's "nuts and berries" complaint about Jen's food choices. It didn't work; instead of teasing Jen for following her preferences, Karen mock-scolded her for violating her principles.

After the meal Karen said, "I'm just going to stick my head in the door. Want to come?"

The unnamed destination Jen knew to be a particular bar, the scene of Karen's social life. Jen declined. When her mother left she went upstairs to the room that had been hers ever since they had moved to this house, when Jen was still a child. She turned on the television, flipped to the channel broadcasting the World Series, and sat down on her bed. Her mind wandered to her room and the changes it had undergone. The present color scheme was earth tones—tan, ivory, green,—but when they first fixed up her room Jen had chosen bright yellow and pale blue. At that time Karen had a boyfriend, a carpenter, who had installed a cabinet for Jen's stuffed animals. A large purple teddy bear named José was the father of all the others. Their family relations had been the constant theme of Jen's solitary play.

Building that cabinet was all the carpenter could do for Jen, because he was married and had children of his own. When Jen moved to Boston, Karen requisitioned the animals' cabinet for use downstairs. José had been relegated to the closet where he remained, in a plastic storage tub, with his progeny and their friends.

Jen brought out José and put him beside her on the bed. She pictured her mother standing in the chilly night outside the bar, smoking, talking in her raspy voice. Part of her wished that her mother was more high-class. Why had Karen slipped from her parents' position on the social scale? On the other hand, Jen admitted to herself, her mother seemed happy and plugged into life in a way that Jen was not—and neither was her snobbish grandmother.

Because her team, the Boston Red Sox, was not playing, Jen watched the ball game in a disinterested, analytical frame of mind, observing the interaction of probabilities with outcomes, which distracted and relaxed her.

In the morning Jen drove to the farm. She hadn't been there since spring, when the kids were only a month old. She wondered whether they were still playful. Jeff opened the front door before Jen knocked. "Barb's in the barn," he said. "Waffles in the kitchen in an hour."

Jen turned to go around the house.

"Thanks for your help yesterday," Jeff added.

Jen smiled and nodded.

The hay-packed loft gave the main floor of the barn a fragrance so strong that Jen imagined herself swimming through it. Opening the door to the dairy, she entered a completely different space, well-lit, smelling of grain and goat and disinfectant, warmed by the friendly woman standing between two nannies. "Do you remember Sissy?" Barb asked. "Sissy, do you remember Jen?" Although she was about the same age as Jen's mother, Barb's skin was rosy and her voice was youthful.

"Sissy had triplets, right?" Jen pictured three reddish-brown little goats.

"Yes, two females and a male, and they all have done well. I'm going to sell them next month. Would you like to milk Sissy?"

"Okay, but you'll have to show me."

Sissy was already in the stanchion, eating grain. Barb cleaned her udders, put a stainless steel bowl beneath them, and showed Jen how to squeeze the milk from top to bottom. When Jen's hand touched the warm flesh of the goat she felt an indecency, as though she was violating Sissy's privacy. Her squeamishness caused her to hesitate. "Sissy likes to be milked," Barb said. "She needs to be milked."

Reassured, Jen began. She thought out loud, "Yesterday Jeff was saying: the soil turned green by the sunlight and the grass turned white by the goat."

"A mammal doing her mammal thing. I think about that."

"Sissy's in the flow of life."

"The nannies keep me from feeling barren," Barb said. "They stand for the buck, give birth, and make milk." She gave quick cleaning squeezes to the nanny in the adjacent stand. "I'll never give milk myself—but in a way I do it through these gals."

"I suppose I won't make milk either," Jen said, squeezing the alternate teats with an increasingly regular rhythm.

"You never know," Barb said. "It's not too late for you."

"It might as well be," Jen replied. She felt no urge to conceive a child and only vaguely wished she had a boyfriend. Jen did not picture herself in the flow of biological life but that didn't disturb her. When she fretted about what she was not, it took the form of a career such as, *I should have been a zoologist*, or a major goal—*I should run a marathon*. She never thought, *I should be a wife and mother.*

As Jen milked the second nanny she wondered how much solar energy spurted into the bowl every time she squeezed a teat. "What's the fat content?" she asked.

"This time of year about four percent," Barb said. "They're winding down. I'll only be milking another month. In nature her milk would be helping the kids get ready for their first winter, supplementing what they were getting from other foods."

"And the protein?"

Barb knew that number, too, and interpreted it in the context of the seasonal cycle of wild goats. Jen listened but at the same time pursued her own train of thought—*sunlight-powered chemical reactions locking energy into molecules.*

Barb, who recognized in Jen the perfect audience for information about goats' natural adaptations, gave that theme its fullest treatment. Jen did mental math; she estimated the amount stored energy passing from the goat's body into the shiny bowl.

When Barb and Jen had finished milking the goats and had released them into the pasture, they returned to the farmhouse. Jeff had cut up fruit, cooked bacon, made waffle batter, and heated the waffle iron. "How are things at the frame shop?" he asked Jen.

Jen washed her hands and considered her answer. "They're okay. The owner isn't there much except when I'm out of town. I've usually got the place to myself, which is good and bad."

"Nobody looking over your shoulder."

"Right—and there's no help when you are trying to do a good job with one customer and somebody else is waiting and they think because they just have a quick question you ought to be able to interrupt what you are doing."

"I can picture it," Barb said. "They hover around and glance at you."

"Right. But the main problem is, am I wasting my life?"

Jeff ladled batter onto the lower surface of the waffle iron. When he closed the top, steam swirled up around its edges into a sunbeam. Jen watched him through the glowing mist.

"We'd all like to know the answer to that," Barb said. "For ourselves, I mean."

Jen thought that Barb and Jeff were in a different place than she was. "You guys have a real life."

Jeff grinned in a way that made Jen wonder if he'd already smoked marijuana. He could be a little high, she thought, or maybe he always seems so, out of habit. Her mother said that the dope Jeff had smoked over the years would fill the barn's hayloft.

"Goats are real, that's for sure," Barb said. "Farming is real and making cheese is real but that doesn't mean this is the way we should be spending our time."

"Me, I'm just framing other people's pictures—"

"And guiding nature trips," Jeff said. "That's pretty cool."

"Yeah. Yeah." Jen looked at the batter that bulged between the curving edges of the waffle iron, and wondered what forces held it in place. It didn't run down the side of the iron as it had when Jeff had first closed the lid. Then she looked out the window at a tree with rich yellow leaves. *Probably a hickory*, she thought.

"Do you want to guide more trips?" Barb asked.

"Anyone would want to," Jen said.

"That's what Barb said the first day she was here," Jeff said.

"What?" Jen was confused.

"The waffle has stopped steaming," Barb said.

"'Anyone would want to,'" Jeff said as he looked at the waffle. "I'll let it get a little browner." He lowered the lid. "The first time she sat at this table she sat right where you are and she said exactly what you just said."

"She wanted to be a guide?"

"No—she wanted to be part of our group. She thought anybody would."

"I wanted to live in this house," Barb said. "And, as it turned out, I've lived here ever since."

Jeff pictured her there on the first morning. At first he had assumed she was just another girl passing through, but after twenty minutes talk at the kitchen table Barb had started working, which set her apart, and six hours later she was still working, which set her far apart. *Cute and helps* had been Jeff's strong impression. Even Elaine had grudgingly approved of Barb, which was the first time Elaine had said anything positive about a newly arrived female.

"I'll never forget her tuna salad," Jeff said. "It was so excellent. She knew how much mayonnaise to use. She put in sweet pickles and laid lettuce on the bread and made everything nice."

"And you fell in love," Jen said.

Jeff nodded and removed the golden waffle from the iron.

"I really appreciate what you said about offering a toast to my dad at the reunion," Jen said.

"Glad to," Jeff said.

"You don't need to do it to make me feel good, though. I just want to know as much about him as I can. I never used to think about him but I find right now I'm curious. It must be something about this particular point in my life." Jen took half of the new waffle. As Jeff ladled more batter onto the iron, Jen noticed the indicator change from green to amber. She wondered where, in the appliance, the designer had placed the temperature sensor, and how it worked, and how accurate it was.

Fresh steam rose into the kitchen. Looking through it, Jeff met Barb's glance. He guessed at her train of thought, *You are going to praise Boomer?* She would recognize the generosity to Jen but be surprised at his insincerity. Jeff remembered Boomer's angry mode; how it made everyone feel unsafe, and his uselessness, when he was a bleary-eyed drug-stupored lump. What drugs had he done? They never asked. It was true, as he had told Jen, that Boomer could come up with knowledge that none of the others had—but the place was happier when he was absent. Fortunately, he had been absent most of the time.

When she returned to her mother's house, Jen asked, "Why don't we have any of my dad's stuff?"

"I got rid of it. He didn't have much. I'm not a saver."

"Why didn't his parents act like grandparents?"

"They did. For a while. But, you know, we weren't married, and they were old fashioned, you might say, and we were never close. Probably Boomer had other girlfriends. I shouldn't say that to you. I didn't always know where he was."

Jen began to cry.

Her mother went to her and hugged her. "I'm sorry, honey. I'm sorry. Really, it was always just us. You and me."

"Yeah, but you had a father," Jen said through her tears.

"Oh, honey. I'm sorry. I messed everything up. I'm sorry." Karen's eyes were wet. "I messed everything up."

"I wish Jeff was my father."

"He wishes he had a daughter like you. I bet he does." Karen released her embrace. "Maybe you wish Barb was your mother?"

"No, Mom."

"Who could blame you?"

"I'm happy you're my mom."

"Be happy, honey. Just be happy. I just want you to be happy."

"Okay, Mom. Okay."

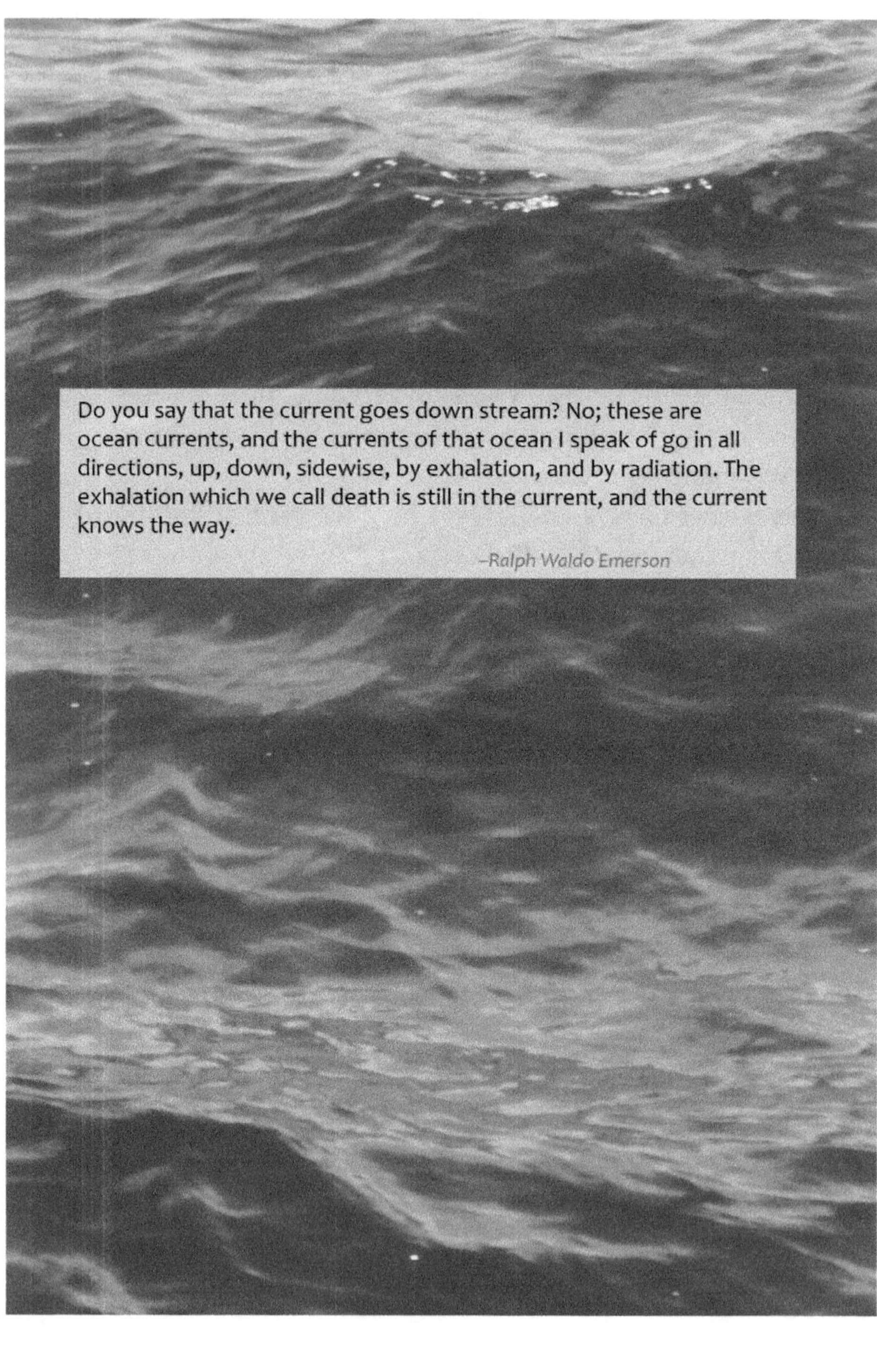
Do you say that the current goes down stream? No; these are ocean currents, and the currents of that ocean I speak of go in all directions, up, down, sidewise, by exhalation, and by radiation. The exhalation which we call death is still in the current, and the current knows the way.
–Ralph Waldo Emerson

6

The day after he failed to sell his company, Bob Quarless met with his lieutenants. He carried a plate of excellent croissants into the conference room. As they went around the table, Bob briefed his managers on the status of the acquisition. Although they had been told about the stall-out, he thought they should get an official version from him. Bob invited suggestions about next steps and found strong support for the "do nothing" option. He thanked his team and adjourned the meeting.

Back in his office, Bob called his mentor. "Skeets? Bob. Lunch?"

"I can't eat lunch. I'd get fat. Walk?"

"Sure."

They met at a university conference center called Mount Sachem, named for the wooded hill that loomed behind the buildings. Skeets McFarland unfolded his long body from his car. He was fifteen years older than Bob, flat-stomached, fit. Skeets was a legend. He was one of the most successful high-tech entrepreneurs around Boston. In semi-retirement, he played music—he was the lead singer and harmonica player for the Blue Hills Bluesmen.

As they climbed the hill, Bob brought Skeets up to date about the attempted sale of Thundercloud, in which Skeets owned a significant interest. "We've hit this bump in the road," Bob said between hard breaths.

"Want my advice?"

"Always."

"Forget this deal."

"What?"

"Get good value or no sale."

"I'd like to do the deal."

"I'd like to protect my investment."

"I'm ready to be done with this."

The men had reached a level area of the trail. Bob's lungs relaxed. He noticed the noise of their steps on the newly fallen leaves.

Skeets changed the subject. "I've got to find a new guitar player."

"What happened to Jerry?"

"Too old."

"You're all old."

"Yeah but Jerry is acting old."

"You're going to kick him out?"

"No, no. Wouldn't want to hurt his feelings. We'll just add a new guy, if I find one, and when Jerry shows up, he can play, too. If he's not sounding good, I'll unplug his guitar. He'll never know."

"How's that?"

"He's deaf."

"Maybe they'll do that to you someday."

"Fair enough."

"You'll be up there singing into the microphone and jiving around like you do and nobody will hear you. They'll hear this other guy behind you whose mike is plugged in."

"I'd look ridiculous and not know it."

"Like Jerry."

"Like most old guys. As long as we're having fun, who cares?"

Bob kicked an acorn. "No worries about your dignity?"

"Dignity! What chance do you have for that with your body and your brain slippin' and slidin'? When you're young you are stupid but your body works great and by the time you're old enough to know what's what, the flesh is unreliable."

If Skeets had unreliable parts, Bob didn't want to know what they were. Where to take the conversation? With most people he would have asked after their kids—but not with Skeets, who had lost both his son and his daughter. So Bob asked about upcoming travel, which gave Skeets plenty to talk about until they completed the three-mile loop and said goodbye.

The next morning Bob woke up wondering whether Ruth was in bed next to him. He listened for her and attempted to remember her schedule. He probed—slowly, with one foot—and found her leg.

Gradually Bob remembered that he was still the boss of Thundercloud Systems. He told himself that he really ought to be focused on the Thundercloud sale, but he had to force himself to think about that. Was he being too passive? He felt that he was apt to watch events as if from offstage, reluctant to act. If you called this patience, it was good—but it was sometimes hard for Bob to distinguish his patience from inertia, timidity, or confusion.

"Are you awake?" Ruth asked.

"Yeah. What are we doing today?"

"It's Saturday. I'm raking."

"Ah."

"You could help."

"Okay."

"We're having supper with Jack and Annie."

"Okay."

"At Renoir's. They will tell us about Belize."

"Let's get landscape guys to rake."

"They don't rake. They use blowers. I'm raking. You don't have to."

Bob sat up and opened his laptop. He hoped that his inbox would contain a message assuring him that Thundercloud was all set, but the list of message-senders did not include his lawyer.

Bob texted his brother, *When is your party?*

Halloween, Jeff responded.

Can we come?

Sure. Still got your wolf mask?

I'll look, Bob wrote. Then he put on his work clothes and went outside and raked.

That night he and Ruth were with Annie and Jack in an expensive restaurant. Reflecting that they could afford anything on the menu, Bob said, "We are the masters."

His wife wasn't sure what he meant. Annie said, "God. We are."

Jack asked what they were talking about.

"We're on top," Annie explained.

"Oh, so this is a guilt thing," Ruth said. "Please leave me out. I'm too tired."

Jack nodded. "You're tired from helping people who make stupid choices. You work hard just to send them back out into the world to do more dumb things."

Annie looked at her husband. "Ruth does great kind work but that doesn't mean that you and I deserve all this."

Jack lifted his menu. "All this?"

Annie made an inclusive sweep of her arm. "All this everything."

"What's *deserve* got to do with anything?" Jack asked. "We're doing our part for the economy, keeping those little electronic value-capsules flowing from one account to another. We spend that others may have income."

"My how times have changed," Bob said. "We didn't make that case in the Sixties, did we? Speaking of which, we're going to the North Road Farm anniversary party."

"I want to write a piece about North Road Farm," Annie said. "I'm going to use the reunion as a setting but it's really about our generation's view of itself."

"Interesting," Ruth said.

"What's your take?" Annie asked.

"All of my takes are boring. Ask Bob."

"Okay Bob," Annie said, "North Road Farm. What did it mean?"

Bob recalled his first visit to the farm in Dutton, when he had been accompanied by his college girlfriend, Pamela, an anthropology major who was lively and adventurous and had been the most enthusiastic of his sexual partners. "It was part of that time," Bob said. "You guys—all of us—wanted to make a better world. There had been so much ugly stuff—the Depression and World War II and the Holocaust just before we were born—then the disgusting white response to civil rights. Then came the War in Vietnam."

"Yeah?"

"It was a dismal pattern. There had to be change. We tried different things. You guys did the commune. Why not? Everything else was corrupt, shallow, no good. So, more power to you or to the spirit of the times that led to that and all the other experiments. That's how I felt then and nothing has changed."

"Why did it fall apart?" Annie asked.

"There were specific circumstances," Jack said.

"The farm could have kept going," Annie said, "after Phil and Elaine sold to Jeff."

"My brother and Barb are nice, generous, excellent," Bob said, "but in the end they are pragmatists, not visionaries."

Jack tapped his index finger on the table. "Our idealism sat next to expectations from the way we were brought up. Underneath, many hippies still valued home and family."

"Is that why you left?" Ruth asked.

"Kinda maybe," Jack said. "For us the farm was a place to hang out for a while—I was in my lost-soul phase, my Indian period, corner hating—"

"Corner-hating?" Ruth looked confused.

"That's why he built a geodesic dome," Annie explained. "To have a place that was round. Like a teepee."

"I built the dome while she," Jack pointed to Annie, "being well organized and mature, wrote her dissertation. And she made photographs. For us it was like the MacDowell Colony or something except that the food was monotonous and the person sitting next to you at the supper table might not smell very good if they were Hoeth or Rubble."

Bob tried to picture those two. "Was Hoeth short?"

"Yes," Annie said. "Rubble was tall and cute."

Bob raised his eyebrows.

"Too young for me of course and besides I was taken," Annie continued. "Your brother was also handsome. The farm had good looking guys."

"We desired to change the world," Bob said, "and we had other desires, too. We were hedonists. And as you remind us the urge to pair up and multiply brought a consequent need to meet expenses."

Annie held her hand out over her plate and rubbed her thumb across her fingers. "And all the time you were in B-school."

Because Bob was accustomed to falling under suspicion of being what the counter-culture had termed a sell-out, hearing that suggestion did not distract him from his own train of thought, which had reverted to Pamela, to a time when hot weather had affected their love-making—they had been covered in perspiration and the skin of their front surfaces smacked when Bob lifted his torso. Pamela had remarked that the word "fuck" might have come from the noise of wet chests separating.

The sun was high when they woke up; the air already heat-heavy. The room they occupied was called "the pantry." It overlooked the road and the driveway and opened to the kitchen.

"Want some cereal?" Pamela asked.

"Okay," Bob said.

Wearing nothing at all, Pamela started toward the door.

"My robe is right there."

Pamela picked up Bob's cotton bathrobe, put her arms into the sleeves, and went into the kitchen. Bob couldn't see whether she closed the robe's front or not, but when she returned with cereal it was tied.

"Cornflakes," Pamela announced. "Banana. Brown sugar. You go back today, right?"

"Yes. My internship starts tomorrow."

"That makes it sound like you're a doctor or something instead of a businessman."

"Internship. A term commonly used for unpaid work."

"Why do that?"

"For learning. You work to learn. And to make contacts."

"Why do you need contacts if you're going to start your own company?"

"You don't do a start-up by yourself. You need help."

"It's a group thing? A capitalist commune?"

"Right."

"Do you think it would be okay if I just stayed here for a while?" Pamela had been working at a summer camp but had been let go. *They had a lot of rules,* she had explained.

"What would you do here?"

"I could write up my field work." Pamela thought of her weeks at the camp as an anthropological study. "You could come out on weekends."

"Maybe. I might have to work."

"On weekends? For nothing?"

"It can be intense. Expectations are high."

"It sounds like bullshit to me." Pamela pulled on a tee shirt that did little to hide her perfect breasts.

Bob watched. He felt detached. He had thought he was in love with her. He didn't ask about her time at the camp; he was worried that he might learn more than he wanted to know. He tried to suppress his jealously of her freedoms; the opportunities she'd had for sex while he had slept alone and written letters to which she had not responded.

Later that week Bob called the farm. "I'm working for this great guy named McFarland," he told Pamela. "He says I don't have to work every weekend so I'll visit sometime soon."

The following weekend Bob couldn't drive west because his car was in the shop. Instead he went to the beach with some others from the business school and their friends. During this outing he had a long conversation with a woman named Ruth Gorley whose boyfriend was traveling in Europe.

Bob had expected to spend Labor Day weekend at the farm with Pamela—but she told him she had plans to "go camping with friends from school" and that she would try to get a ride into Cambridge the week after.

That autumn Bob still felt attached to Pamela. She sometimes joined him in Cambridge, where they heard music and went to restaurants—on Bob's nickel. One evening, wishing to clarify their plans, Bob called the farm. His brother answered.

"It's Bob. How the hell are you?"

"Good, man," Jeff sounded a little nervous.

"What's going on?" Bob asked.

"Not much, you know, same old. You looking for Pam?"

"Yeah. Is she handy?"

"No, she and everybody but me went to Northampton to the movies."

"Okay—"

"But it's good you called because I kind of wanted to talk a minute."

"Sure man. What's happening?"

"Well, it's funny, I don't know what to say exactly, but I don't think Pamela is, like, the most true-blue girlfriend you ever had. I mean she's nice and all, I like her, but being your brother I just feel like I should say that she's a little out there sometimes. I don't know."

"Is she shacking up with other guys—is that what you mean?"

"Not as far as I know—but I wouldn't say it couldn't happen. She's best buddies with Elaine—I guess you know that."

"No, I didn't realize that."

"Yeah. Which is fine, but there's other stuff."

"Has she come on to you?"

"Not exactly, no, but maybe I've kind of had the feeling she was hinting along those lines sometimes. Maybe I misunderstood and that wasn't even true at all."

"Yeah, well, anyway, I appreciate you mentioning it. I think for her it's like when we're together we're together and when we're apart that's her own business. I think that's her deal and I better like it or lump it."

"You coming out for Halloween?"

"Maybe. I'm invited to a party here, too."

"If you came here we could be the Werewolf Quarless Twins. If you still have your mask."

"Same here if you came to Cambridge. If the timing works out right maybe we could terrorize both parties."

"Maybe I shouldn't have said that stuff about Pamela," Jeff said. "I don't know why I did."

"You didn't want me to get blindsided. I appreciate it."

The night Bob and Ruth dined with Annie and Jack, Jen was at home by herself. She lived in an apartment in a carriage house in a Boston suburb called Westforest. Jen couldn't have afforded market-rate rent for her place; she paid some money and helped her landlords, an affluent couple named Eastman, who lived in the main house. Jen was sometimes their babysitter, pet sitter, and hostess helper. To Jen the duty seemed light compared to the benefit of living here in a town with abundant conservation land. The Eastmans, who were younger than Jen, never asked so much that she felt imposed upon. Jen liked their two little girls. The over-all package worked for her.

Jen sat hunched over a piece of graph paper writing with a pencil. She loved graph paper, and used it to make personal budgets and lists of birds she'd seen or heard and for various plans and designs. One design she spent time on was her Earth Emigration Vehicle—a device to carry humanity's descendants on a long voyage through space. Jen tried not to think of the passengers as people but she also didn't think of them as robots. She imagined that they were advanced far beyond her time but still made of flesh and blood—and their intelligence was based on human language.

Jen considered this activity to be a form of play, in which some planet-destroying catastrophe loomed, and Earth's inhabitants needed to take their civilization elsewhere. The project motivated her to learn. She took courses online and she sought out engineers and scientists to query. Those people had no idea who she was or why she asked

such odd questions but most of them were willing to respond. Jen
wanted to understand the future energy requirements for maintaining
intelligence, the spore of culture, over long periods of time and
space—there would be dormancy and reawakening. After civilization
had been somehow encysted, what would trigger its emergence?

Jen filled binders with her plans and designs—indexed them
with care, kept her pencils sharp, made graphs and drawings—often
in front of a baseball game, discussing them with no one.

As she was musing about whether her plans should include
lower forms of terrestrial life, Jen received a text from Paul Scribner.
Looking forward to the old people?

Jen replied, *?*

At North Road Farm.

Oh! The Halloween party.

Yeah. You're going?

I told Mom I would.

I'm glad. It will be nice to see you.

Laura's going, right?

She's got other plans.

Too bad.

No biggie. See you.

Jen wondered, briefly, why Laura would not be at the party—
but she was accustomed to not quite understanding other people's
choices and feelings; she felt mild surprise but was not distracted for
long. She took in the fact that Paul would be at the farm by himself,
then she turned her attention to baseball and to the quantity of bean
flour to be stowed in the Earth Emigration Vehicle and the diameter,
in kilometers, of the reflector needed to thaw food with starlight—
unless, as the vehicle coasted through the galaxy, perhaps heat could
be harvested from one gravity system's rub against another. Jen
picked up a pencil.

Love and self reliance balance up and down, and the beam never rests.
–Ralph Waldo Emerson

7

Annie turned on her computer. As it booted she looked around her office. Her eyes fell on souvenirs from trips. She picked up the jade turtle she used as a worry stone—she cradled it in her hand and rubbed its belly with her thumb. She rearranged two Zuni fetishes—a raven carrying a coral berry, and a bear inlaid with turquoise.

Some bills lay on her work table. She had paid them electronically—now she filed them. When the table was clear, she opened her closet, revealing a shelf of loose-leaf notebooks, carefully labeled—Annie was disciplined about organizing her photographs. She looked for a binder that was on the far right—the end of the shelf that held the oldest material. It was labeled "Dutton 1974-75."

From a cabinet Annie took a small light box, its power cord, and the loupe she used for examining slides, negatives, and contact sheets. She lifted the lid of her scanner and inserted a frame to hold strips of negatives on the machine's glass bed. Then she opened the binder and removed a group of negatives and their corresponding contact sheet. Although Annie appreciated the tidiness of digital photography, the physicality of real film pleased her and took her back to when her hair had been dark and plentiful and decades of future adulthood had stretched beyond her mental horizon.

When Annie was young, darkrooms remained in their heyday; the imminence of their demise entirely unsuspected. The equipment, materials, and procedures of the darkroom were, at that time, essential to making pictures. Like all other photographers, Annie had learned to use her sense of touch to wind exposed film into a light-proof canister—an operation that required total darkness. Once inside the container the film could be bathed in chemicals that developed and fixed the images. After it had been rinsed and dried, the film was cut into strips that were laid side-by-side on a sheet of photo paper, then exposed to enough light to transfer the image to the paper. When developed, fixed, washed, and dried, the paper showed a small positive print of each picture. From these contact sheets the photographer decided which negatives to enlarge.

Seeing the initials A.L.B. on the corner of the contact sheet reminded Annie of a joke she'd had with herself—that A.L. could stand for Available Light as well as for her given name, Ann Louise. Using only light incident to the scene yielded a more natural picture than if the photographer used a flash. Low-light photography resulted in grayer, grainier images—a look Annie thought added authenticity and artiness. She had eschewed the flash and relied on whatever light happened to be falling on the subject.

Annie removed the contact sheet from its plastic cover and bent to sniff it. She had a keen sense of smell and habitually established context for thoughts and observations through her nose. The paper retained some sweet acidic darkroom odor that reminded Annie of working in dim amber light. She had learned her way around darkrooms in high school and spent many college hours within them. She recalled a particular afternoon with a student who was in her photography class. Annie and he both had steady lovers at the time— but she and this guy liked each other. They were seniors, getting ready to move on. They joked in class in a friendly way, not explicitly flirtatious—but a mutual appreciation had been established.

Late in the term they decided to share a darkroom session. They told themselves this would be practical but as soon as they had turned on the darkroom-in-use sign, which warned others not to open the door, Annie had sensed, in herself and in her friend, a certain excitement. As he and she took turns making enlargements they chatted in the amiable humorous tone that had led them to companionship. The physical closeness, darkness, and occasional brushings of one's clothing against the other's created an amorous mood. When the young man slid a certain print into the tray of developer, he said, "This one's of you. You look so great."

In response, Annie had found a posture and an angle of her face that conveyed *so kiss me*—and he had. The result was a heated frenzy.

They tried to muffle their excitement in case there were listeners outside.

Eventually they had re-opened the door to the world, cleaned up the darkroom, and gone their separate ways. The spontaneity and intensity of their love-making crystallized in a bond that, because the rest of their lives were spent apart, existed only in memory. The guy, Annie knew from the alumni magazine, had married his girlfriend and learned to fly and they and their children had died in a crash.

Annie had never mentioned that darkroom sex to her college boyfriend, nor to Jack who had been her next boyfriend and whom she had married. The incident was a secret she carried. Its recollection brought a certain exaltation that she wished always to protect.

Through her loupe, Annie looked at the first image on the contact sheet. It showed the back and shoulders of a shirtless man, outdoors. The next was from his front—Rubble with a post-hole digger. Fair hair fell around his smile. His muscles looked good. In the series of shots he went back to work, hoisting the double-bladed tool, thrusting it into the hole. Annie could imagine the sound it made slicing through sandy soil—and recalled the chink when it hit a rock.

What would he have said to her as she took his picture? When she and Jack had first visited the farm, this young fellow had caught Annie's eye. He was younger than they—an exuberant boy—lacking intellectual confidence but radiating animal energy. Between the beginning of their visits during winter, and June, when Jack and Annie had moved to the farm, Hoeth had arrived, taken Rubble for her own, and restored his given name of Duane. It had been clear to Annie that Hoeth was prepared to defended her claim to her boyfriend with every weapon at her disposal. Remembering that the two had worked all summer to fence the pasture, Annie wondered whether the goats now used the same field. Did those fence posts, planted by Rubble, remain in service?

A second figure appeared in the background, reminding Annie that Hoeth was seldom out of earshot when a female was close enough to talk to her boyfriend. Except for Elaine. Hoeth didn't worry about Elaine.

In the next group of pictures Jack staked the location for the geodesic dome he planned to build. Then came a series of people preparing supper in the kitchen. The last few exposures on the roll Jack had taken of her. She was on a chair in their room at the farmhouse. She had been looking out the window toward the road. Seeing the four images of her in her T-shirt—two were poorly focused—she remembered Jack asking if she would take off her clothes. *For you but not for the camera,* had been her response.

Annie withdrew the strip of exposures of Rubble, alias Duane, from its clingy sleeve. To avoid smearing oil from her fingers on the negative—photography teachers had instilled a dread of that—she handled the negative by its edges. She put the strip into the frame on her scanner, lowered the lid, and made digital images of the best exposures.

The next roll of film began with Boomer leering at the camera, his tongue obscenely projected. Seeing his face, Annie recalled her relief when he had been killed. She thought he had abused Karen. Sometimes he had been earnestly helpful; he could be a puppy-dog, anxious to please. He had wanted to help Jack solve problems with constructing the dome. Jack preferred to figure things out for himself but he recognized Boomer's wish to connect with him over building something and tried to accept. A picture showed them mixing concrete for one of the footings. Annie had a sudden wish to be in Dutton, on the farm. She picked up the phone.

When Barb accepted her call, Annie asked if she could visit.

Barb said that very day would be good although Jeff would be at work.

Annie decided that it was still early enough to make the drive. A few hours later, before knocking at the house, she walked to the dome. She was surprised at how small it was.

Barb and Annie took chairs at the kitchen table. "How well I remember sitting here," Annie said. "Brown rice and lentils. And meetings. Oh my god the meetings. I don't know why Jack and I haven't been more in touch."

"You're on the North Shore." Barb said. "That's a long way from Dutton."

"Even without traffic. I'm glad you are having this party."

"You said you wanted to get some history," Barb said. "Are you making a scrapbook or memory book or something?"

"It will be a slideshow. And I'm planning to write an article."

"I forgot you're a writer."

"Mostly I am a teacher of writing but I try to maintain my credibility with a piece from time to time. In this case I'm taking our youthful aspirations as my topic."

"How can I help?"

"Do you remember when you moved in?"

"While you were on your way out here I dug this up." Barb opened her diary. "It tells exactly when I arrived—January 25, 1975. I wrote that I could hear you typing in your room, the front room. Remind me what were you writing."

"My PhD dissertation. French literature. What were your first impressions?"

"I wanted to know whether Jeff had a girlfriend!" Barb laughed. "What a relief that he didn't! All the people here interested me—but especially him."

"Was Boomer dead yet?"

"No, but the accident happened not long after."

"I always wondered," Annie said, "whether it was completely an accident."

"Really?"

"I suppose it was but because I was pretty sure he had raised his hand to Karen and I hated that so much I projected somebody killing him. Maybe I wanted to."

"He was on his motorcycle in the rain."

"Yeah but that didn't mean he had to run into that concrete. He went off the road at so exactly the right time."

"You think somebody ran him off? Who are your suspects?"

"I don't know," Annie said. "I'm just playing mystery writer. Maybe some guy felt sorry for her."

"I think Jeff did feel sorry for her. But I—"

"Well, whatever happened it went down as an accident and no doubt it was," Annie said. "The guy was not really a part of things here—but Karen was."

"It's all so sad," Barb said. "Then Karen had that dear kid. And the kid never saw her dad and it hurts her very much."

"We've just been birding in Belize with Jen. She is hurting?"

"She seems sad to me. Smart, sad, lonely." Barb described Jen in the goat barn and repeated her remark about life flowing through the nanny.

"This should really be a play," Annie said.

"What?"

"It could be. A play. Then and now. Karen and Jen. My guy Jack building a dome for everyone to get stoned in and Jeff, your guy, taking care of practical stuff and Philip with endless group process—"

"And Elaine."

"Elaine. Wow." Annie looked around. "It was all her money, wasn't it?"

"What was?"

"Everything. There was no North Road Farm without Elaine's beer money. And she had the moral drive. Her edge." Annie remembered how she had felt listening to Elaine at meetings—a mixture of gratitude for her aggressive feminism and resentment of her patronizing tone. "We were just learning the word 'assertive,'" Annie said. "That was good—but Elaine was self-righteous like the politicos. She was why our group couldn't grow."

"You had to put up with her to stick around," Barb said. "You didn't have to agree with everything but it was great that she was strong about women's lib. Everyone buys into it now but they didn't then."

Annie nodded. "She made it easy for you and me to seem reasonable. She changed Jack, that's for sure. He didn't want Elaine on his case."

"I don't know if she changed Jeff or not because I didn't get the before-and-after view. I know she appointed herself his co-carpenter that first summer. Were you here when she had the baby?"

"Yes. That was a trip. Over there," Annie pointed toward the broom closet, "sat strange Pamela the pseudo anthropologist doing magical weirdness in support of the birthing. Driving the midwife nuts." Annie reflected that the midwife, at the time, had seemed old, but now she realized that the woman had been in her thirties.

Elaine had cursed at the top of her lungs during contractions. After each contraction she closed her eyes and whispered, "Bastard, you bastard, you bastard, oh fuck," then fell silent.

Philip, Annie remembered, had worn a surgical mask. He had offered one to Pamela who had pretended to accept it then let it parachute to the floor.

"I photographed the delivery," Annie said. "I had never seen a baby being born. It was a huge experience for me."

"Was Jeff in the room?" Barb asked.

"No. He wasn't here. I suppose he was at work."

"Well. He and I have delivered many babies but they are all goats."

Annie laughed. "Thank you for finding your diary. What else have you got?"

The dates and events Barb had recorded covered the commune's dissolution—the departures of everyone but Jeff and her. "You could talk to Karen about earlier stuff. And Jeff. You might be able to catch Karen today because she's right here in Dutton and I think this is her day off."

Annie drove to the address Barb gave her. She found Karen on her porch; the weather was warm for October.

"Remember me?" Annie asked.

Karen shook her head.

"I'm Annie Brown and we lived together on the North Road Farm for a while."

"Oh yeah." Karen waved Annie onto the porch. "Now I recognize you. Hello!"

"I just was over with Barb talking about the old days and I wonder if I could come by some time and see what you remember."

"What's wrong with now?"

"Now's okay with me," Annie sat down. "I'm doing a little writing about our generation. Do you miss those times?"

"No," Karen said, "Except the music. The music was great."

"Yes ."

"I've never been the same since Janis died."

"Janis Joplin. It was awful that she died so young."

"I'd like to come back as her in my next life."

"I think for me, Joan Baez."

"That would be cool. Want a beer?"

When they both had a beer, Annie asked, "You moved to the farm with your boyfriend?"

"Kinda maybe." Karen lit a cigarette. "He was off somewhere—Boomer—when I moved in. When he was around, he was there with me. Good old Boomer."

"Do you have any favorite memories from the farm?"

Karen laughed. "The chickens. I always liked the chickens. They were funny. But mostly it was just a place to hang out, as good as any I guess."

"You and Elaine were pregnant at the same time, right?"

"I was a few months behind her."

"Did you have some friendship around that?"

"Around what?"

"Both being pregnant?"

"Oh no. Hell no. Not even close. She was a major bra-burner. That was okay, but . . . she had that nutty pal, Jeff's brother's girlfriend, hanging onto her about how she should have that baby at the farm without drugs or anything. Not me; I wanted a nice doctor and nurse and all the drugs I could get."

"I know your daughter. I was with Jen in Belize. She's an outstanding naturalist."

"Smart kid. Always was a smart kid."

"Yes."

"I guess she got it from her grandparents. Skipped a generation, the brains. Oh well. She puts up with me most of the time."

Annie took a deep breath. "She never met her father."

Karen's features hardened. "No."

"That's too bad."

"Yeah, well, I don't know what kind of father he would have made. He was kind of a . . . he was not perfect."

"He hit you?"

"Yeah, sometimes, but mainly I've come to realize he was just generally inconsiderate. That's what I'd call it, overall. Inconsiderate."

"Did he have PTSD?"

"Huh?"

"He was in Vietnam, right? I thought maybe he had post-traumatic stress disorder."

"Of course he blamed everything on 'Nam and the army. What the hell good did that do anybody?"

"Right."

Karen stabbed out her cigarette. "Another thing that was great about the farm wasn't the food."

Both women laughed.

"You didn't go there for the food unless you were, like, a vegan or something," Karen said.

"There's excellent vegetarian food now," Annie said, "but we didn't know how to do it back then."

"Even being stoned didn't give that crap any flavor," Karen said. "But Jack made good popcorn." She looked at Annie, watchful for signs in her expression that would warn her away from the topic of Jack. "Are you still with him?"

Annie nodded.

"I remember listening to music in his dome."

"He ran an extension cord out there," Annie said. "When the weather was just right. If it was raining there were leaks. If it was sunny the dome was too hot, and most of the rest of the time it was too cold."

"It was great, though. Listening to the Dead or the Velvet Underground or whatever. Smoking good herb."

I wonder if I have pictures of that? Annie thought. "What about the others?" she asked. "Did you really have a hard time with Elaine?"

"Elaine and me? We did all right. We were just totally different and you know we both have a mouth so neither of us was like kidding anybody that we were friends or anything but I respected her because she said what she thought—she wasn't some princess popular or anything."

"Maybe I seemed like a princess popular?"

Karen snorted. "You were like the one person who seemed to have her stuff together."

"The happy graduate student finishing her degree."

"With a nice boyfriend, yeah, and you kind of kept to yourself. I couldn't tell what you were thinking. That's what I remember. You kept an eye on everybody but didn't say much."

"That sounds like me."

"You probably thought I was a low-rent hippie chick."

"What woman in those days didn't fantasize about riding off behind a guy on a big Harley? And you really did it. I felt like I was stuck being a little middle class good girl, locked inside her comfort zone, while women like you were out there."

"I was. I was out there all right."

Annie let the pause become a longish silence.

Finally Karen said, "I liked that tall kid. What was his girlfriend's name? Something weird . . . "

"Hoeth. She moved in just before Jack and me."

"Funny name. Hoeth. That girl landed on the tall kid like a hobo on a ham sandwich. Those two liked to work. And they liked to eat. And I seem to recall they liked to screw. I'd wake up in the morning and they were already out there doing something, planting the garden or whatever, and then a couple of hours later you couldn't find them and we figured out they were off somewhere taking a fuck-break, and then the next thing you knew they were splitting firewood."

"What did you think about Phil?"

"He was okay. He was the chief, him and Jeff, and somebody had to be, I guess. Of course he was under Elaine's thumb but so what? At meetings I kept quiet. He would listen to you and Jack because you were intelligent."

"Were there people he didn't listen to?"

"I guess not. He was fair."

"I always thought he really did want to hear what everybody had to say."

"I probably wish I'd had more to say. Remember that time Hoeth wanted to put up clotheslines? There already was a clothesline but it wasn't long enough and she had this whole plan about how much we needed and how to hold it up and where to put it so they could use it in the winter—we were getting a washing machine—remember that?—until then we'd gone to the laundromat in town, I guess—and Hoeth not only had a vision for the clotheslines, she also did not want the drier that Elaine and Phil thought, because of the baby coming, we had to have, and she, Hoeth, had Rubble say—she'd given him his orders, I guess—she had him say or at least he did keep saying 'We ought to save energy.' Remember that?"

Annie had not remembered that but as Karen described it she thought maybe Jack had suggested that they skip the washer, too, and take dirty clothes to the bottom of the hill and wash them in the stream and then they wouldn't need the washer *or* the drier. Annie pictured Jack, maybe it was after that or maybe it was some other meeting, rolling his eyes and asking her in the privacy of their room if she wouldn't prefer a nice house somewhere where they could cook steaks or bacon and do whatever they wanted without having to hear everybody's opinion about everything.

That disconnect—the distance between normal suburban independence and the way they lived on the farm—brought to mind the jolt they felt when Jeff took them to a concert at Greylock Music Center. Classical music had been important in Jack's and Annie's families, but the Beatles, Rolling Stones, Doors, and the Jefferson Airplane had displaced Mozart and his ilk as far as they were concerned. At Greylock they could see that the old world—the pre-Civil Rights Movement pre-Vietnam pre-counter-culture pre-Woodstock pre-LSD universe was not about to go away. Annie had been surprised to observe that the audience—the affluent aging New Yorkers and Bostonians—behaved as though nothing had changed. Their dress, the ways they wore their hair, and their assured demeanors suggested that their old world had not budged—which shocked the young adults from North Road Farm.

What had they expected? That the scene at Greylock would include giant amplifiers on the stage and marijuana in the breeze? Instead they heard an orchestra of aging white men play for an audience of complacent white grandparents. Maybe nothing *had* changed. "Do you think there's been any progress?" Annie asked.

Karen didn't know what she was talking about.

"We thought our generation would change the world. At least that's what I thought."

"And here we are all these years later and dope is still illegal," Karen said.

"But we have an African-American president."

"True."

"Want to see some pictures?"

"Sure."

Annie opened her laptop on the coffee table in Karen's living room.

"What are we looking at here?" Karen asked.

"Photographs I took at the farm."

The picture of Duane with the post-hole digger appeared on the screen. "He was a good kid," Karen said.

"And cute," Annie added.

Karen guffawed. "It'll be nice to see him again. Barb says they're both coming."

Annie clicked to a photo of Hoeth. "Not too pretty in this picture but I never thought about that at the time. She was energetic."

"Yeah, it was, when you were living with somebody, it was all about, what were they like to live with? It was a pretty good bunch on the whole. Have you talked to Elaine?"

"About the farm you mean?"

"Right."

"Not yet."

"I think she went gay. When she left Phil I think there was a woman in the deal somewhere."

"Okay, look at this one." The screen showed a face painted like a zebra's. "Who's that?"

""What's this? Halloween?"

"Yes." The zebra stood in the middle of a room with others seated in the background. The whole picture was dark; the white stripes were gray. "Who is she? What were we doing?"

Karen squinted. "I'll tell you what that was. I know what was happening. Remember 'Murder in the Dark?'"

"No."

"Yes you do. It was that game we loved to play."

"Okay."

"Remember? We drew slips and someone was the killer and someone was the cop?"

"Okay." Annie began to recall. They had played fairly often. At night. The detective had to sit still in the dark until someone screamed. Then he or she started turning on lights, hunting for the body, and trying to see who was where.

"The zebra was the cop," Karen said. "You must have been taking pictures during her investigation."

"How did you ever figure that out?"

"I don't know. It just came into my head. That happens sometimes. The give-away is Phil lying on the floor. He's the corpse."

Karen identified the zebra as a woman from Kipling House—the Vermont group that had come down for the Halloween party. The next few pictures were other angles of the living room. Between Karen and Annie they were able to identify each person. Duane and Hoeth had paper bags over their heads. Jack was wearing a Richard Nixon mask.

"Who's missing?" Annie asked.

"You are," Karen said. "Because you are taking the pictures. And there is Phil but no Elaine."

"And where were you? And Jeff?"

Karen wore a startled expression. "Hmm. Well, there's kind of a story there. Because, well, I remember that night, that party—I guess it was that party—well, maybe I shouldn't say."

"Shouldn't say what?"

"Why maybe Jeff and I weren't in the pictures."

"There's no Barb either."

"There's no Barb because there was no Barb at the farm yet, no Barb in Jeff's life, see. He was still up for grabs."

"Oh."

"And Boomer was gone and tell you the truth I always had kind of a thing for Jeff."

"Did you?"

"Yeah and this one time during the game—and I can't believe it was the time you took these pictures but I suppose it was because I know I was there—I remember the zebra girl and the other costumes—I decided to hide in Phil and Elaine's bedroom closet. I went into it and there was already somebody in there. Jeff. It was cozy and sexy and you know—we were really drunk or stoned or plenty of each. Anyway I think we stayed in that closet through the investigation or at least well into it. I think I came back late to the living room or else the game ended then, that was the last round—people went to bed and I, like, listened to music and did some dishes or whatever—with that feeling I got sometimes that I wished Boomer would stay away and Jeff would love me."

Annie didn't say anything.

"But Boomer came back and then he got killed and did stay away." Karen was crying. "But by then Barb had come and she was perfect for Jeff—even I could tell that—and it was too late for me and besides I was pregnant."

"With Jen."

"Yeah. She's the only time I was ever pregnant. Which is pretty amazing when you think about it . . . the odds."

"So that's how it happened . . . "

An angry look suffused Karen's face. Annie said, "I just mean—"

"I know what you mean. You mean if I got it on with Jeff in the closet why couldn't he be Jen's father." Karen's anger melted in the face of Annie's evident kindness. Tears returned. "Yeah, how many times have I had that thought? But I'm not sure that what happened in the closet could have made a kid. And Jeff never said anything about that night and Barb came and Boomer came back and then got killed and, fuck it, I know Jen's mine and it always felt right to put that out of my mind and let well enough alone." She wept.

Annie moved beside her on the couch and put an arm around her.

"Jeff and I had done it once before—I can't believe I'm telling you all this—at the farm, but before you and Jack were there, on Valentine's Day we got close but he never wanted me for his woman the way I wanted him and that wasn't fair anyway because I didn't get rid of Boomer—I'm not sure I would have known how—and when Jeff and I talked I ended up feeling like I wasn't good enough for him and then after the closet thing he was like nothing happened so why put it on him or give him the satisfaction or whatever so I just went home and had my baby."

"After Boomer died you went home?"

"Yeah, eventually. I wasn't going to be like Elaine and I was ready to be done with North Road though I did come back here to Dutton after all."

"You liked the town."

"It was a good place for Jenny to grow up."

"It's a nice town."

"It's been good to us. And I got the job with the town so I didn't have to live off my dad and got this house and things have gone okay."

"Yeah."

"I mean I ought to stop smoking and lose weight and all that but, hey, I never claimed to be perfect. Just another aging hippie chick." They sat in silence until Karen said, "Jesus. It was life. It was our life. What can you say? The music was great."

As she started her car for the long drive home, Annie noticed a wave of feeling. She envied Karen's acceptance of her flaws. Annie accused herself of trying to be perfect—her talents and circumstances left few excuses. Despite what she had said to Karen, she didn't attempt to be good-girl perfect; she tried for live-fully perfect.

Annie placed her restlessness on her mental table, in good light, to look it over. What was her problem? She compared her life to Barb's and to Karen's. Because Annie was closer to Boston and Cambridge she had more cultural opportunities—but how often, really, did she use them? In the Berkshires they had real New England towns. Dutton was the genuine article—and Karen and Barb and Jeff were part of Dutton in a way that Annie was not part of her town. Forbes was a geographical place and a provider of services. It offered the Brown-Bigelows an attractive setting for their good life and provided amenities—top schools and library, excellent Fourth of July fireworks, and a Unitarian church with a smart, ironic minister. Town politics were reasonably civil. *We do have everything,* Annie thought. Coastal Coffee served beautiful lattes. The supermarket catered to those conscious of health and nutrition.

Annie itemized her cares. She'd had one cancer scare and was jittery before every mammogram. Her parents refused to move into assisted living. Her husband liked his alcohol a little more than he ought to. But overall Annie could see how smoothly the road of her life was paved.

Did she picture herself in Forbes forever? The good life was great, and boring. Yes, she loved her husband but they had been a couple so long it was unfair to expect him to excite her. Their love-making had a ritualistic quality. If not for hormone therapy she wasn't sure she would still enjoy sex. *Maybe I should have an affair.* She knew she could tempt a man—the problem was that she didn't know anyone interesting enough to bother with.

I love my husband. What did that mean? She and Jack shared a droll companionship. His quirks and unconscious little slights she could overlook. Jack would not be trouble, had never been trouble, in any of the ways a man could be a serious nuisance. He watched a lot of movies and television—but he had to pass the time somehow, and not everyone read as much as she did. Her husband was like the rest of her life—comfortable.

Annie considered herself lucky to be with Jack—she knew many women would wish for what she had. What was missing? Nothing unexpected, no fresh challenge—the same old hat—a well-fitting adequate hat—but was one hat enough for the rest of her journey?

Why not try on something else? Annie made an effort to imagine a suitable guy. Couldn't there be a man whose body was hard where Jack's was soft; who was still ambitious to compete and to achieve; who had strong opinions he loved to defend? He would want Annie to challenge his thinking so he could show his stuff. He would invite her to accompany him to adventurous destinations. He might persuade her to back-pack in bear country—that would take her out of her comfort zone. His sex would be aggressive—but he would be tender before and after his intensity.

Or perhaps she could find a man who would lead her on a mental journey into deep new learning and self-realization. An ingenious creative man—a high priest of something that mattered.

Annie didn't know any men like those she imagined. Besides, she thought, fantasies left out everything you did not want, whereas reality would bring those unwelcome extras.

Annie had no wish to hurt Jack. He did not know about the times she had cheated: first, before they were married, with a professor, her advisor in graduate school, and then a few years later, when she herself was the teacher and had a fling with a student's husband. After that she had settled into monogamy. She told herself that if she needed new interests and stimulations she should find them in her work.

That resolution took her thoughts back to what she would write about the farm—and to her notion about its theatrical potential. She pictured the set—the farmhouse kitchen. The play could open with the childbirth scene. At the edge of the stage, Phil, in a white spotlight, was on the phone with his physician father. Perhaps she'd put the doctor there, too, representing the Establishment's virtue—a middle-aged man kindly disposed, vaguely puzzled by the times, astonished that an educated woman, his own daughter-in-law, would attempt to bear a child at home.

Annie's photographs of the childbirth had authenticity; they said, yes, this was us; this really happened. Elaine had always been a force. Annie wondered why she did not have more memories about Elaine from the time at the farm. An answer occurred to her—*because I avoid conflict.* Having watched her older sister attempt to shock and displease their parents, Annie had made herself the easier daughter. She had done whatever she wished but had not insisted that her parents know about it—and they had not been nosy.

Annie observed that, over the years of her adulthood, she had gained a sense of her own ground and felt that she could stand well-balanced upon it. She could afford to hear what others had to say. For that growth she credited her relationship with Jack. His interest in her point of view had increased her confidence. That was part of why she could say *I love my husband*—because their countless little conversations had brought her to a good place with respect to herself. She wondered if she had given him the same benefit.

Annie had been impressed by Karen. On the highway, in Karen's honor, Annie listened to Janis Joplin. She wondered whether the guys in the Holding Company were still alive, decades after they had been abandoned by their singer, who had died, at the top of her fame, from an overdose of drugs.

When she got home Annie emailed Elaine. They met the following evening at a bar in Somerville. Annie wasn't sure she would recognize her, but she did, by a familiar hint of swagger.

When they were seated Elaine asked, "Who have you interviewed so far?"

"Karen and Barb. Jeff was at work."

"Talk to Jeff by himself. That goes for each person. I will be a fly on the wall when you interview Philip."

"Oh?"

"Things between us have always been fraught, but Phil is a good guy, you know, a nicer person than I'll ever be or ever wanted to be, and the world is better off with some niceness even though it's not my thing."

"You were always direct which is different than not nice."

"It's nice of you to say that but I don't think most people would agree because niceness inherently means biting your tongue or else pre-spinning what you have to say so it will not alarm the other person."

No rebuttal occurred to Annie.

"I'm a city girl," Elaine continued. "A country commune was a funny thing for me to get involved with. But it was exactly what we did back then, wasn't it? If my nice young husband and his friend wanted to buy a farm out in the sticks, who was I to say no?"

"Who indeed. You're from the Midwest, right?

"St. Louis."

"How did you meet Phil?"

"At college. Tufts."

"Did you think of yourself as a hippie or a student activist or what?"

"I thought hippies were mindless. They *were* mindless. Deliberately. Turn on. Drop out. I thought of myself as a radical. The big thing to me was SDS and all that."

"The political part."

"Correct."

"The civil rights movement had a huge effect on me."

"Civil rights and segregation put everybody in the country on the spot," Elaine said. "Because an African-American woman worked in our house, I had a close-up view. My parents thought they were respectful of Tulie. They imagined that by giving her a little extra money sometimes, like at Christmas or when she had to go to the doctor, that made them generous. Here they were, as rich as anybody in St. Louis—not a high bar, in the big world, but they were definitely in the ruling class of that small city and Tulie kept everything going in our house. She *helped my mother*—that was the euphemism people used, which meant, did all the work. Little Elaine wondered, 'Who keeps Tulie's house?' because it couldn't have been Tulie—she was at our place all the time. I asked my mother, *who does Tulie's housework?* My mother said, 'Her people live simply,' or something like that—the tone was, *don't worry; they're fine* and the connotation, *who knows?—not our problem.* Mom would have used the phrase 'her people' to place Tulie in the dark-skinned caste and to separate her group from our group.

"I could observe the power structure right there in my own family. Not just because of Tulie, either. People would come to see my father, leading people, and they would speak to him with deference. I knew early on that old Dad wasn't the brightest bulb in the shed; my mother was the brains of the family. They deferred to his power and his penis. I'm running on. You want to know about the farm."

"You bought the place, right? I mean, really, it was you?"

"Yeah, little old me with my little old trust fund," Elaine replied. "Philip and I had gotten married—a barefoot wedding—I had hippie-like tendencies sometimes—who didn't want to spite her mother? And then the next year Phil and his pal Jeff decided to buy a farm where we'd all do our back-to-the-earth collectivist thing so they found the place and all I did, really, was put up the money."

"You weren't into it? Into the group farm thing?"

"Oh yeah—I was—that's how we were going to resist the system. Drop out. Turn on. Tune in. We did plenty of turning on, that's for sure. I don't think the system noticed that we were gone. I was more of a mind to blow up the system, to go on the attack, but the guys, my guys at that time, weren't the attacking kind. They were sweet. I wasn't sweet. I hope not. But the farm was. The Berkshires and growing food and acting friendly to the straight neighbors. The kind of revolution our guys wanted would be painless. We were so naive— and I must have been the most naive of all."

"Why do you say that?"

"Because I truly believed that something in this society would change and nothing did."

"Didn't all the major radicals switch sides and become stockbrokers or something?"

"Hell no! I'm sorry but I hate it when people say that. Those guys you are talking about were power-lust sexual pigs who were always white male bastards. No surprises there. Show me the feminist leader who switched sides or budged a bit. We took up the struggle and we've kept at it."

"I see your point. Sorry. And you don't think our society has gotten any better?"

"Not much," Elaine said. "Maybe a little, in limited ways. Very little."

"Looking back on it, those times were complicated."

"They were."

"What would you identify as the components?"

"The Resistance, the Movement, that was first and foremost to me. And then there was sex, drugs, rock 'n roll—of course I liked all that like everybody else. There were others: back-to-the-earth, environmentalism, Eastern religion, meditation, group process—they were smaller but still important. They were part of the cultural tidal wave and they were major to some people like Jeff and Phil. For me the big thing was the Movement—first the political left in general and then more specifically the Women's Movement which disabused me of admiring some of the supposedly radical guys. That's been my thing and if you want to know the truth it's been by far the most important. Maybe you disagree."

"No—I wouldn't disagree." Annie had complete sympathy with the underlying goal of Elaine's politics: a society that was fair and offered public kindness. A society in which violence of every form was held to the minimal level necessary to protect people from would-be oppressors or destroyers. At the same time, Annie was repelled by bureaucracy, by monopoly, and by those forms of regulation designed to provide little fiefdoms to autocratic personalities. With respect to the extreme end of the Movement prized by Elaine, Annie had not trusted the dogmatic my-way-or-the-highway tone adopted by its leaders. There was plenty to be angry about—but talk of bombs and revolutions seemed, to Annie, out-of-place and harmful in a country that had reasonably open political discourse.

Annie was conscious of valuing enterprise, initiative, and some decent balance of individualism with collectivism. Although she had convinced herself she was ready to debate such matters with Elaine, to clarify their areas of agreement and disagreement, she decided not to go there now; it wasn't why they were talking. She wondered, *What if Lyndon Johnson had continued his war on poverty instead of switching to the war in Vietnam? Would not the sixties have ended much differently?*

Rather than hear Elaine disparage that line of thought, Annie took the focus back to North Road. She asked, "Concretely, when you think of your years on the farm, what comes to mind?"

"Let's see. Making Jeff let me nail shingles. We worked together on the new roof. Having my son. And the dome."

"The dome?"

"Yes because it was in the dome that I first realized my feelings for Pamela. Or, no, maybe that's where I first knew that she returned them."

"Pamela?"

"Sure."

"Ah."

"You never caught on to that?"

"Can't say I did."

"I was still trying to figure out what I wanted. And having Paul and whatnot. And Pam was, at least officially, still dating Jeff's brother. She was actually finished with him. Christ, he was in business school. Can you believe it? How could you come out of the sixties and want to go to business school? But—he did—Bob did."

"Full disclosure. Jack and I are friends with Bob and Ruth."

"Aha. Well, full disclosure, I'm still lovers with Pamela."

"Are you?"

"Yes and I think she can come to the party."

"Does Bob know that?"

"I don't think she and Bob have communicated. And I'm not sure she's coming—she tends to keep her options open."

"She wasn't at the farm all that long, right?"

"No but she was there for Paul's birth. She was part of that. By then I think I was finished with men. With, as I say, occasional exceptions. For Phil, who is an unusually decent man."

"Speaking of guys—I've been trying to remember what I could about Boomer."

"Now there was an argument for being done with guys."

"You didn't like him?"

"He was your basic unreconstructed insensitive woman-beating sexist pig."

"Can you cut him any slack for PTSD?"

"From Vietnam? Not really—not me. Make him a victim? No. Think about what he probably did to people over there. They'd have been very lucky to pull through with only PTSD. No. To me, Boomer was a perp."

"Back to the big question: don't you think Tulie would get a fairer shake today than she did when you were little?"

"Oh god. I don't know. I hope so. I doubt it, but I hope so."

What does not vary is the necessity for man to exist in the world, to
be at work there, to be there in the midst of other people, and to be
mortal there.

–Jean Paul Sartre

8

Bob was still in his pajamas, reading the news on his laptop when his phone rang. He was in the room he called the porch. Ruth referred to it as the atrium—it was enclosed on three sides by thermal windows. Although it was chilly outdoors, Bob was perfectly comfortable in his robe and flip-flops because morning sun poured into the room.

Bob's phone displayed "Stewart McFarland." Bob swiped to accept the call and said, "Hello Skeets."

"Bob. It's Skeets."

"Yes. What's up?"

"Fair is fair; just giving you advance notice.

"Of?"

"I will be in touch with my fellow board members."

"Thundercloud board members?"

"Yes, your board members. I don't like what I'm hearing about the sale."

"I don't recall you voicing enthusiasm at any point."

"Right, and now its worse because it's obvious their stock is going to keep slipping and we aren't going to end up with what you promised."

"I'm listening."

"I've been consistent, right? If I was ever going to make an exception it would be for you."

"Skeets, I'm going to get this deal done in the way that will be best for everyone."

"Maybe. There's a chance it would work out that way. A remote chance. What you will actually be doing, whether you can admit it or not, is doing what's best for Bob. That's natural enough but you've never been able to admit it. Because of your hippie background."

"I was a piss-poor hippie."

Skeets told Bob he would lobby the board to cancel the deal based on the projected low value of the purchaser's falling stock.

"Skeets. Don't do this."

"You'll thank me in the end."

"No I won't."

"Whether you will or not, be advised, I'm taking steps."

"Thanks for the heads up."

"Any time. Every time."

The call ended. Bob watched a squirrel on the lawn. He tried to figure out what it was doing. The actions of this ordinary creature were mysterious when closely watched. Did it hold any intention in its minuscule head? Or did its body merely run one rote procedure after another?

God damn it Skeets.

After sending Jay Phelps an email describing the call, Bob tried to go back to reading the paper. He felt like Lebanon—a well-disposed country between stubborn antagonists. He thought about all that could go horribly wrong in the Middle East and that it probably would, or inevitably would, given enough time. He reflected, *These are the good years*—when many of the world's people lived in decent security with enough to eat and hopes for the future; with the illusion that things would get better, but Bob thought they were far more likely to get worse, to be undermined by disease, bad weather, automatic weapons, bio-terrorism. Death to America was the menacing chant—as though America didn't have enough killers of its own.

A cat wandered into the room. Because its eyes were in front, it projected more smarts than the squirrel. *Because it looks more like us,* Bob thought.

Bob stood up and put his computer on a table. The house was empty except for him and the cat. Ruth was at work. At certain moments Bob envied Ruth for having a job that made its own meaning. People with injuries or illness needed her help. At the same time, he knew that no career that put you on a treadmill could have worked for him. He needed projects with strategies, risks, life cycles, and outcomes. Bob's callings were, jointly, to service and to power. Early on he had decided that the most direct service was provided by creating jobs—that the difference between prosperous places and hopeless places was that the prosperous places had jobs. So the best thing you could do for your community was to hire people. Bob decided to become a starter of businesses in the computer industry not only because it looked important but because the code-puzzles of programming were, to young Bob, fun.

In college he had majored in linguistics, not with a view to an advanced degree but rather with an intense pursuit of understanding; it was the human capacity for language that had given us dominion. Then came business school and being mentored in entrepreneurship by Skeets McFarland himself—Boston's premier high-tech guru, who had advised Bob to head west, to California, to set up shop. Bob supposed that to be the only piece of Skeets's early advice he had ignored. He took a pass on earthquakes, wildfires, and mudslides. For Bob the advantage of New England was the way it had been sitting there for four hundred years, thinking. Something about stone walls, colonial houses, and old Yankees were a comfort. New England had, for Bob, a calming effect.

He called his brother. "I'm screwed," he informed Jeff. He explained his situation.

"Oh man," Jeff said. "Everybody thinks it's easy being a billionaire."

Bob's net worth, even after the most wildly successful sale of his company, would have had no proximity to that figure. Jeff used billion to indicate a vast sum. Anything higher than ten million seemed pretty close to a billion to Jeff. Bob was well attuned to the many increments of value between the proposed sale of his company and a billion dollars, but, in reply to his brother, he merely grunted.

Jeff changed the subject. He thought that the best comfort he could offer was normal conversation. "Annie Brown was out here talking to Barb the other day. She said she'd just seen you."

"True. What was she doing out there?"

"She's doing slides for the reunion. She's being a honeybee, flying around to the old North Roaders to gather their stuff."

Bob noticed he wasn't caring much about what Jeff was saying. "I hate it when my problems get to seem like a big deal."

"Yesterday Annie texted Barb that Elaine might bring Pamela to the party."

"Pamela?"

"That's right."

"Oh! Well. I wonder what she's been up to. I guess we might find out."

"We might. Annie's coming back," Jeff said. "She wants to see inside Jack's dome. I'm going to get that cleared out."

"What's in there?"

"Packaging. Milk bottles. Canning jars. Dairy stuff we haven't used and probably never will use. I think Barb's all finished with the raw milk business."

"Cheese is better?"

"Safer, easier, more profitable."

"How's work?"

"My work? Fine. Thank god for musicians and people who pay to hear them."

"I'll drink to that. Speaking of which, it's time I got started."

"Not really, right?"

"Right—not really."

After the call, Jeff went out to the barn. Jeff liked his brother, and he liked the fact that their relationship immunized him from feeling like a hick.

When Jeff had moved to North Road Farm, his adulthood had been all before him. He had arrived with his girlfriend, Carol, but she had not loved the farm and their relationship had faltered. She went home for the holidays and never returned. Hurting, young Jeff found three points to steady himself—his growing carpentry skills, his friendship with elderly neighbors Sam and Rebecca Regal, and the physical presence of the barn.

Jeff loved the way the barn told its own history—especially the shop, with hardware piled on the work bench and, on the dark boards of the walls, steel gate hinges, horseshoes, and chains. The steel spoke to him; its heft, the depth of its cold, its defiance of time, its mysterious provenance. Shapes of steel had been joined to wood or leather that had after many years released these screws and bolts and harness rings. Although Jeff had never seen live horses in this barn, he could hear their ghosts stamp and snort.

Jeff stood in the barn's shop, looking at the workbench. North-facing windows filled the room with mild blue light. It seemed the same to Jeff as it had forty years before—the smell, the colors of the oil-stained boards. When he had first stood at the bench he had not realized that this was where he would live his life. North Road Farm had invited Jeff to put it to rights, to repair, recover, and preserve. He had hungered to anchor here—to connect with reality in a way that no college course, nor any other school experience, had offered. He remembered how, during a visit with the neighbors down the hill, Rebecca had held up her liver-spotted hands and remarked, "You and I live through these. Lucky people, fortunate people, live through their hands."

The first time she said that, Jeff had reflected on the counterculture maxim, *Don't trust anyone over thirty.* So wrong.

Rebecca had taken up the same theme during Jeff's next visit. "Hands bathe the baby. Pick the berries. Knit the scarf," she had chanted. What had she been doing? Making pies? Jeff remembered her in full production during blueberry season. Or perhaps she'd stood in the small greenhouse that jutted from her kitchen—starting seeds, or, later in the season, dividing bulbs. In the greenhouse she talked about the milk snake that often appeared there. "I call him Pete because Sam always says *for Pete's sake.* A milk snake is good luck."

She might have been on her knees in her garden, pulling weeds, echoing the mew of the catbird each time it called. She told Jeff how, during the war when their kids were little, she'd wanted a cow. Sam had discouraged the idea but, "when a chance came along I got one and brought her home. She was a sweet cow and she gave us a lot of milk. Sam lives through his head. Sam's got a good head and the whole town benefits, but for him it means fretsome worries. We're lucky, you and I, because we think with our hands."

At Greylock, in the early years at his job, Jeff had allowed himself to be seen as one of the blue-collar workers. He played down his college degree and played up his readiness to learn from the people around him—the unschooled dignified men who had their own simplicities and prejudices but who tried to be open to new views. These men showed Jeff how to use tools and helped him understand the strengths and vulnerabilities of trees and their relation to soil and light. From Jeff the men learned that a kid with long hair could show up, work hard, give and take respect, and participate in much, but not all, of their humor. Because of Jeff's quiet disapproval, the frequency of racial jokes gradually declined after he joined the crew.

Due to his love of the barn, his body well-made for work, his job, and his friendship with the neighbors, Jeff settled into life in Dutton more thoroughly than any of the other North Road farmers. Although country life suited him well, he did not wish to feel like a rube—that's where his connection with his high-tech start-up brother served him well. His clear view of Greater Boston affluence left Jeff pleased with what he had in the Berkshires and unenvious of metropolitan amenities.

Where, in this barn, could the junk in the dome be stashed while their guests were here? The main space was out—that was party central. The dairy would be in use. Jeff rejected the idea of piling stuff in the shop—it would be in his way if he needed to do anything. That left only the loft.

Jeff crossed the yard, looked into the dome at the volume of cartons to be moved, and sighed. *If Jack wants this thing cleared out,* he thought, *Jack can empty it himself.*

What is the substance of elegance but the will to serve all?

–*Ralph Waldo Emerson*

9

When Annie met Philip for lunch, she asked him how he had chosen his profession.

"I passed some kids at recess on the way over here," he replied. "Think back to starting school as a little kid. They drop you into a crowd of strangers. Most could act normal but some could not—they exhibited strangeness. The teacher didn't seem surprised by furious outbursts. Uncontrolled behavior shocked me but I could tell that teachers expected a certain amount of craziness. Interesting!"

"First-grade chaos destined you to become a mental health professional? Nothing to do with the sixties?"

"The sixties? That too. But first, before then, I think about us playing soldiers and cowboys-and-Indians around the neighborhood, watching television, hearing that the Russians were going to bomb us or take over the country or both. Oh man."

"The Cuban Missile Crisis."

"Right. My parents put some canned goods in the basement and said that was our fall-out shelter. There we were between Ozzie and Harriet and atom bombs. No wonder so many decided to live for the moment. I was a do-gooder. I thought, how can I be helpful? I chose to become a therapist because the suffering among people I actually knew came from their minds. The other stuff, bad as it was, was at a distance. Mental health problems were in my face."

"You could see that at school."

"There was a boy in my first grade class who really couldn't function, couldn't manage himself. It was as though he was possessed. This was before there was much special ed. That kid intrigued and frightened me. Reading and doing math seemed pretty straightforward, but people were something else. Difficult to understand. And in the neighborhood—I heard the man and woman next door shouting at each other. Enraged. I wanted to make sense of it all. Didn't you?"

"Sure."

"Of course you did and you turned to literature and the stories people tell and you compared what it felt like to be you to what they said, the writer said, it felt like to be others."

Annie looked at her hands. "That's a fair way of putting it."

"But me, I wanted science. Science had figured out so much about the world. My father was a doctor and everything he did was based on science. He told me there was this new-ish science, psychology, about people's brains, and I thought, that's for me. I looked it up in the World Book Encyclopedia—the entry on psychology. Gradually I realized that psychologists were still trying to figure out how to apply the scientific method to human predicaments. There was this guy named Freud and this other guy named Jung and now this character Skinner and none of them agreed about anything. Some smart people believed in each of them. But believing in isn't what scientists do, is it?

"I wanted to help people find ways out of their emotional pain. It would have been nice if there could have been a theory, a model, like physics or chemistry, of what caused people to feel awful and crazy and hopeless. But instead there was a search—and I could be part of it."

"We were all searching," Annie said. "How can we make sense of the world? How can we feel okay in it? What is worth doing?"

"Yes yes yes. And who to do it with? Elaine and I shared the excitement at first, although we ended up pointing our flashlights in different directions. That was predictable—we are both so intense. I can't for the life of me remember why we thought it was a good idea to get married. We were too young to marry."

"You've never remarried."

"Not yet! Maybe I will. Or maybe not. Once on the *Jack Paar Show*, I saw something that stuck in my mind. I was a kid—thirteen or fourteen—and Paar asked some writer why he had never married—a middle-aged guy — and he responded that he loved all women too much to marry any one of them. There was applause. I, a kid, didn't understand that the guy was gay and the applause was a knowing approval of his diplomacy. What he said works more literally for me, a straight guy who's been married and had a series of deeply-loved women friends. Some lovers; some not."

"Your original interest in people has stayed with you."

"That has no end."

"And you have helped many people, and still do."

"Maybe. It is hard for a talk-therapist to know how much difference he makes. You have to acknowledge that the brain chemistry stuff and the medications have concrete results that you seldom see with talk. I'm more of a teacher and people don't learn my stuff very fast."

"What stuff do you mean?"

"Relatedness. People feel okay in proportion to the quality and quantity of their bonds with others; that's the premise. I teach people how to say things that nurture healthy relationships. People shrivel their bonds and become isolated because they do three bad things."

"Which are?"

"Belittle, reproach, and control. Taken together, they form the desiccating voice. The nourishing voice appreciates, encourages, and liberates. I'm sounding so didactic; my process is not one of precepts — that approach fails. Persons have to discover such notions for themselves to make them useful. Or I should say, I have found that to be the case for individuals who are habitual desiccators."

"When we were in Dutton together, was that already your approach?"

"No. That grew over the years. But my readings at the farm — they certainly laid the groundwork for all of my thinking and my approach to my work. When I think of the farm, I think of *The Whole Earth Catalog*? Remember that?"

"Of course."

"And the wonderful subtitle, 'Access to Tools.' Steward Brand—what a head. Jeff had every issue of *The Whole Earth Catalog* and he seemed to have memorized them all. I had read books about group living experiments. We were drawn to the rural idea. Back to the soil. Communal living. I was married to a socialist. Putting all this together it made sense to buy the place in Dutton and have some people live there."

"And Jeff still does live there after all these years."

"Yeah, he was more the farmer whereas for me those years were an immersion in group process and what it meant to be married to Elaine and to become a father in a family—a feminist family. That was huge for me. At those morning meetings—that was where I really got to try to create an accepting environment like Carl Rogers wrote about."

"You practiced group therapy on the farm."

"Yes in the sense of trying to offer unconditional positive regard, in the Rogerian phrase. For me the farm was about ideas—and— remember the old apple orchard?"

"Sort of. Was it uphill from the pasture?"

"Yes. Those old trees were full of holes. Holy trees—my joke to myself—I could find a spiritual feeling there. My sacred grove. Somehow to me it made sense to put ideas into the hollows."

"How?"

"I typed out thoughts that struck me. From whatever I was reading. Then I crumpled them into balls and left them inside the trees."

Annie smiled.

Philip laughed. "Even then it seemed kind of silly. I've never told anyone and I had forgotten all about it. But now I can remember being up there by myself in the twilight, and re-reading some notion, and leaving it inside a tree."

"What kinds of things did you read?"

"I wanted to be a psychologist, so Elaine gave me William James books as presents. The old couple down the hill gave some Emerson to Jeff. I read that. And poetry. Maybe Whitman. I don't know."

"I always pictured you as intellectual," Annie said, "although I never knew you were doing so much reading. It seems funny that you and I didn't talk more than we did."

"I thought about you far more than you knew," Philip said. "You were beautiful, and remain so. I was married and funny-looking and not the most macho guy on the farm."

Karen would agree, thought Annie, but she herself was drawn to Philip's active mind. "Speaking of macho, remember Karen's guy Boomer?" Annie asked. "Jack and I were on a birding trip with their daughter Jen who grieves that she grew up fatherless—"

"Yes."

"—and then I was remembering Karen's bruises—"

"Yes."

"—and trying to go back to what—"

"The whole subject of Boomer is a painful memory," Philip said. "I had no idea how to deal with him."

"Did you feel it was on you?"

"Certainly."

"Why?"

"I thought of myself as a leader—the responsible person. I tried to monitor everyone's state of well-being. But I was just a young guy. I wasn't ready for real life as represented by a guy like Boomer."

"*Go with the flow* didn't work."

"Right. That's another way to look at our generation—we thought we had it together but we didn't. We were just like every other generation except there were more of us and we caught one technological wave after another—"

"Such as?"

"Television. Polio vaccine."

"Birth control pills," Annie added. "Transistor radios."

"Space travel."

"Digital cameras."

"Digital everything."

"Why did you leave the farm?"

"When we had Paul my focus shifted. I had been chief of the tribe, trying to keep the group pulled together"—he held up intertwined fingers to show the weaving image he had in mind—"and then suddenly here's this baby. Elaine couldn't or didn't want to feed him much so I researched that and talked to the pediatrician and bought the best kind of formula, which unfortunately was made by a corporation not politically correct, which Elaine, had she known, would have forbidden."

"How could she not know?"

"I brought the formula in from the trunk of our car early in the morning, when Elaine was asleep. As you might recall, the farmhouse had one of those dirt-floored cellars, spider heaven, with narrow rickety stairs. Elaine never went down."

Annie shuddered. "Neither did I."

"So I stored the cans there. Then, after the two a.m. feeding, which I always did, I emptied cans for the next day into jars, and put them in the fridge.

"Where did Elaine think it came from?

"She wasn't that interested. Maybe she didn't want to know. Were there goats in the barn? Maybe she thought I milked them. Anyway, I had a major new responsibility named Paul. Suddenly I was an adult, wow, and Elaine's parents and my parents were wondering how I was going to make a living, and Elaine was mad because they all assumed that I was designated bread-winner."

"Ah."

"But on some level she assumed the same and so did I. Never mind she had resources—none of us thought I should be a sponge. I needed to finish my PhD and get certified and start a practice. When I looked around at the farm, everyone seemed younger than I. Because they were still playing their back-to-the-earth fantasy."

"Suddenly it seemed like a fantasy?"

"Like a good fantasy and I had bought into it before but now for me it was over. Suddenly I was a young father."

"What did you do?"

"Elaine and I made it possible for Jeff and Barb to buy the farm."

"That was nice of you."

"Or a better way of putting it is, they made it possible for us to vamoose without having to sell to a developer or something. It seemed to me that Jeff and Barb were so naturally the owners of the place and time has proven that to be true."

"At some point you broke up with Elaine."

"She became deeply involved in the women's movement. She came, after the birth of our son, to identify herself as bi-sexual and she fell in love with a series of women. We moved on down the currents of our lives. By the way, I'm sorry to hear you describe Karen's daughter as grieving."

"Did you ever wonder whether Boomer was really her father?"

"I always assumed that somebody else was Jen's father."

"Why?"

"I was pretty sure Boomer liked heroin and usually guys who shoot up don't care much about sex."

"Oh."

"And Karen stepped out sometimes, when Boomer wasn't around. No mystery about that."

"Well, I, for example never knew she did."

"I guess my supposition was founded on one incident which, as it happened, was with Jeff, but that was before Barb came along. Which takes us back to the sixties and our belief that we had invented sex."

"Not me. I did my dissertation on *Madame Bovary*."

After her long talk with Phil, the thought occurred to Annie that, if she decided to have an affair, he was interesting enough and admirable enough to take as a lover. But, she realized, he wasn't cute enough. She blushed at her shallowness. She was forced to recognize the strength of good looks as a criterion for mate selection—which she had no choice but to accept as a truth about herself, although it embarrassed her.

A few days later Annie received an envelope in the mail, addressed in longhand. It was from Jeff— a letter, in neat script, on lined yellow paper.

Dear Annie,

Your email said you were gathering memories of the commune days and ideas about what they meant to us and what we think our generation has achieved or failed to achieve. I know I told you I'd sit down with you but I decided to respond in writing.

For me the commune years have two big pieces—pre-Barb and post-Barb. The single biggest thing in my life is Barb because I love her so much and our life together is my life. I like my job and other stuff but the main thing I like is being Barb's husband. To go chronologically I'll begin with the pre-Barb period.

As you know, Carol and I and Phil and Elaine were the first to move into the old farmhouse on North Road. All the money came from Elaine and Phil. Why didn't I feel like a freeloader? They bought the place—so what? If I'd had money I would have done the same so it didn't matter. After a few decades as an adult with money often at the center of everyone's attention we think that must have always been true but it wasn't. What I wanted was real life. I'd had this totally white-bread childhood, you know, Dick and Jane and the recent war that the dads didn't talk about and the other important reality topics adults avoided—race, sex, and whatnot. Things were deliberately artificial in the nineteen-fifties. Phil and I wanted to get to something real and living on a farm seemed the way to go.

When we got here the first thing that hit me was the huge need to learn. The house had been described as a "handy-man's dream"; we found out what that meant. And at the same time we changed the phrase to handy-person's dream because women's lib had sunk in; no gender stereotypes for us, certainly not with Elaine around. Phil cooked and Elaine helped me replace the roof. Of course we didn't know how to do any of that stuff so we learned by reading and doing and talking to people, which I enjoyed.

Carol just wasn't into it. I guess I needed her more than she needed me—I don't know. There was a feeling of slipping apart and nothing I could do about it—I felt helpless. That word "possessive" was in the air. I wasn't supposed to be possessive and I didn't want to be but I really liked to be with her and didn't want it to end. Except for losing Carol those were good times—challenging but good. I found out I could do real things and do them well enough to get by. I'm talking about working on the house and barn, teaming up with Elaine and Duane to keep the place from falling apart.

The buildings themselves—wow. Over a century old then and now past a hundred-fifty. For me the house and barn were time travel. I grew up in a new-construction suburban house—ugh! I loved having a house that was old when my grandfather had been born. Just looking at the boards and the nails that went so far back—it got my imagination going about who had touched them, people long dead—the turning of the wheel—those nails were hammered by some person's eyes and hands and tools. Maybe that hammer is still around but the hands and eyes are gone and now my hands and eyes are at another point on the endless turning.

One thing we can say about our generation is we tend to be Baby Boomer Exceptionalists—we thought we'd live on a higher plane of consciousness than our predecessors—but the old farm's continuity—the old farm in the old town—undercuts the idea that we were so different. I came to feel that we were just the latest in the process, the current phase. Our value on being frank and candid— we called it being up front—was a change from how we had been brought up. Still, as I got to know our neighbors I realized that our values were not new.

Sam and Rebecca Regal lived in the house down the hill during the first ten years I lived on North Road. They'd been there much longer than that; they had raised their family there. When we first moved in Phil and I went down to introduce ourselves. Sam and Rebecca were more than friendly. I spent a lot of time there, especially after Carol left. I never felt myself to be on a higher plane of consciousness than they were; on the contrary. Compared to them, plenty of people in our generation look shallow. For example, we thought we owned the anti-war movement. Ha! Sam and Rebecca were Quakers. They had ALWAYS been for peace, and not just because they didn't want to get drafted.

Did we think we should live close to the Earth? Sam and Rebecca had a huge organic garden—they canned and froze as much of their own food as they could. They knew all the birds and the animals' tracks. They felt that they were part of nature. Sam kept bees— that's how I got into it. He didn't care too much about the honey— although Rebecca baked with it. What Sam loved was the way the bees connected him to plants, to his surroundings.

I began to help Sam with his hives—I had a strong back and he had all the knowledge. He taught me the concept of the bee space—the distance bees need between their combs. By giving bees that three-eighths of an inch, they could be persuaded to make combs in wooden frames that could be removed from the hive, de-capped, and spun to release their honey. Each cell in the comb slants up just enough—too many details—but it was all so beautiful and Sam had it all in his head.

Whenever I worked with him he told stories about people he'd known—men and women—I wish I had recorded them. I did record a few. And he talked about Maine—that's where he'd grown up, way up in the woods when there were still log drives every spring. And town meeting—he was a selectman. He described the characters who kept everyone annoyed, honest, and entertained. He knew the strengths and weaknesses of democracy; he lived in it.

And then there was Rebecca. She was totally a person who thought for herself. She spent one hundred percent of her time and energy on what seemed important to her. Her ancestors were Yankees, mostly, but she claimed an Italian grandfather—that grandmother had been shunned by her family for marrying a foreigner, presumably Catholic who had educated himself and done well in management jobs for railroads. Rebecca remembered his voice, with its Italian lilt, reading fairy tales to her on rainy afternoons.

Rebecca claimed to believe in reincarnation. She told me, "I'm coming back as a kingfisher—when I'm gone and you hear that kingfisher rattle—that'll be me!"

Another thing about Sam and Rebecca was that they seemed to like us. And why not? How great were the farmers? The big kid Duane whom we called Rubble—he was lovable. Philip and Elaine, I learned so much from. I guess Phil will always be my best friend if you don't count my wife and my brother. Karen was great and is great—comfortable in her own skin; excellent.

For me though, when Barb came through the back door into the kitchen and asked if I was Philip and I said, "No, I'll get him, and she said, "Who are you?" and we just sat down at the table and talked for an hour before Phil came in—since that hour I'm a happy guy. Annie, that night when no one else could hear, you told me, "Watch out! You two look like a couple." You always had good vision.

Okay. North Road Farm. The counter-culture. Our generation. How to make sense out of the whole thing? Our dads, lots of them, were in World War II. The war was more than enough reality for them, I guess, so they created nice safe suburbs, middle-class paradise. We came out of that needing authenticity, not war if we could help it; more like eggs from chickens you knew, and cheese from milk from goats you loved. It's been my life, really, and I do feel so fortunate.

As for our generation, well, we inherited more tools than our parents had, and we've added to the kit. Computers and the Internet, obviously. And what about the liberation movements? They have changed everything and nothing. We are not smarter or better than Sam and Rebecca. Our consciousness is not higher than theirs and it never was. But they were unusual individuals; they didn't necessarily represent their generation—but who's to say that any of us does?

We used to admonish each other to "Keep the faith." What did we mean? I'm not sure we really meant anything; maybe we just liked the way it sounded. But looking back on it, I guess it's how we expressed the vague hope that life would get better and freer and more okay for more and more people. I guess that's still what we want.

That's all I'll write today, Annie, but I look forward to talking about this with people when they come here. Thanks for getting us thinking.

Jeff

Jen read, *Can we do Waban's?* It was a text from Paul.

She responded, *Why?*

Before each of the trips they had led, Jen and Paul had talked and planned as they hiked up to Waban's Lookout, a granite outcropping high on a hillside. But no trip was currently in the offing.

Debrief Belize, Paul wrote. *Tell you some news.*

What's the news?

I'll tell you in person.

Jen emerged from her car with a bag containing curried chicken salad sandwiches and potato chips. Paul was putting bottles of iced tea into his day pack along with the napkins that he expected Jen to have forgotten. As he gently placed the sandwiches on top, she said, "What's the news?"

"Laura and I have decided to break up."

"Why?"

"It's just not working."

"Really?"

They headed up the trail.

"I think it's hard for her, my issues."

"What issues?"

"Oh, you know. Occasional low spirits."

"I didn't know you got low spirits."

"I don't like it to show."

"Are you moving out?"

"No. Laura is. She's gone."

"Wow."

"I always thought maybe you and I—"

"No."

"No? No what?"

"I'm sorry. I should have let you finish."

"I thought we could go out on a date."

"That wouldn't be a good idea."

"Why not?" Paul asked.

"It's not just the incest taboo—although that plays into it; we are the North Road Farm siblings. I couldn't date you because it's not the way I feel about you and it's not what I'm looking for in my life right now. I've always admired you but in a different way."

"Is there somebody else?

"No."

"Are you some kind of nun?"

"I don't know—maybe I am. It's really my own business."

"Sorry."

They climbed in silence for a while.

Finally Jen said, "I'm sorry if you're hurting but hooking up with me isn't the answer."

"What would be the answer?"

"Well, when I think about it, it's kind of funny because we both—I guess I should speak for myself—I'm missing one parent and I'm not very happy about it sometimes."

"I guess you are blaming my problems on my mother. My mom's a feminist mom, that's for sure. Always has been. That's okay. My problem is this country."

"America?"

"Yes. These people are completely crazy and it makes me crazy. That I can't do anything about it. Apparently nobody can."

"You think we're more messed up than other countries?"

"I don't know. Is water skiing a big deal in any other countries?"

"Water skiing?"

They had reached the smooth granite upon which Waban might have taken his ease before King Philip's War. They removed their shoes and sat where they could sink their bare feet into dark green moss. Opening the pack, Paul said, "The so-called sport of water skiing. Consider it." He handed Jen a bottle of iced tea. "First you get a boat with a powerful engine. Does this boat ever do productive work? It does not. It is called a pleasure craft."

"Could I have my sandwich please?"

Paul handed her the bag. "You persuade some person to get into the water, attach boards to his or her feet, and give them a rope. The boat driver guns the engine. The victim is jerked upright and skidded across the lake to the accompaniment of thunderous noise. Between the noise and the motion, tranquility is destroyed, above and below the surface. A disgusting, pointless, activity."

"Well, Paul, some people like to water ski. Just because you don't like it—do you think that means they shouldn't?"

"They shouldn't because we're all trying to conserve fossil fuel and all those gasoline-powered boats are the opposite of conservation: egregious unnecessary consumption. But the president can't go on television and say that."

"Sure he could if he thought it." Jen handed Paul a sandwich.

"No he couldn't because of number eleven on the American Bill of Rights—the right to be in noisy motion. Think snowmobiles. Dirt bikes. Four-wheelers. Jet-skis!

"Jet skis are pretty bad. But some people use snowmobiles for their jobs."

Paul took a bite from his sandwich.

"We all hate waste," Jen said.

"The callous disregard—that makes me crazy." His shoulders slumped. "Or it's just the way I am."

Jen said, "What about jet planes?"

"What about them?"

"They use fossil fuel."

"True but it is not pointless motion-noise like jet skis."

"People don't have to fly to central America to run up their life-lists."

"If everybody stayed home international relations would deteriorate. The only tourists would be military."

"That's a stretch."

"It's true though. Every hour people spend with people from other countries, war becomes less likely."

"Could I have my napkin?"

"You already have it. It's sticking out of your shirt pocket."

"I had this yin-yang brother-sister thing in my head where I was dad-less and you were more or less motherless but I guess that's not true."

"True, Elaine would be more interested in me if I were black or an exposer of corporate secrets or a woman trapped in a man's body. That's a given. Or if I'd made my mark in some field—she would probably respect that."

"You're the best all-around naturalist in Massachusetts."

"Give me a break."

"You are right up there. Who's better?"

"I could name five."

"It would be highly debatable."

"What about you?" Paul said. "You could be one of the best or the best, if you worked at it."

"I should."

"Back to where we started: why don't we see what we could do together?"

"We lead trips together," Jen replied. "It's good. Don't let's spoil it."

"Okay. Don't say I didn't try."

When she got back to her car, Jen checked her phone. She had a voicemail from Annie asking if she would be willing to help prepare a slide show about North Road Farm.

Barb provided Annie with email addresses of those planning to attend the North Road Farm reunion. Annie asked everyone to scan and send pictures from the commune days. Guests were not limited to those who had lived at the farm—many were people from Northampton and Amherst and Brattleboro who had come to parties on the farm and had invited the farmers to their own social happenings.

In response to Annie's request, a padded envelope arrived from Vermont. Because he had learned to roast his own coffee, one of the Brattleboro men had been known as McBean, which became the brand of his coffee and, later, the name of his chain of coffee shops. McBean was a college dropout who loved hallucinogens and home movies. The envelope he sent contained two rolls of super-8 movie film, each in a plastic canister three inches across and a half-inch thick. The film was accompanied by a note: "Annie how the hell are you? This was labeled N.Rd so maybe there's stuff you can use. Good luck! See you in Dutton. McBean"

Annie found a photo store that could convert old movies into computer files. When Annie opened the resulting digital video, there was Hoeth mugging at the camera. The frame pulled back to show her pointing at Duane, who was splitting firewood. The camera panned until the barn and farmhouse came into view.

The next shot showed people in Halloween costumes, throwing a football, running in slow motion, miming instant replays. Annie remembered watching this from the farmhouse through the window above her desk. Then she had seen Elaine put a suitcase into her car and return to the house. Annie had intercepted her in the living room. "Are you leaving?"

"Yes."

"Are you going to miss the party?"

"Philip has been talking with Dr. Dad," Elaine said, "And I am told authoritatively that drinking or smoking would hurt the baby."

"Uh oh."

"So Pamela and I plan a weekend at Niagara Falls."

"Pamela's going with you?"

"She is."

"You'll miss the grand opening of Jack's dome."

"It will still be there when we get back. Maybe I'll move in there." Elaine pointed to her abdomen. "Maybe I'll have this baby in there. That would be a grand opening."

"Truly." Suddenly Annie wanted a cigarette but decided to wait until Elaine had left. Back in their bedroom she looked at Jack, who sat on the bed reading a newspaper. "Elaine and Pam are skipping the party."

"Without Elaine, merriness increases! Too bad losing Pam though."

"Because she's sexy?"

"Kooky but kind of hot, don't you think?"

Annie made a face intended to express *Maybe so but what do I care?* Leaving Jack to his reading, she lit a cigarette and returned to her desk.

Looking up through the window, Annie saw McBean point his movie camera at the comical football game. *Did I really remember that, she wondered, or did I just imagine having seen it, nearly forty years later, watching this movie?*

When Jen arrived they sat down in Annie's living room. Jen's eyes went to the artwork, which she complimented.

"Some pictures have been in the family and some are by friends," Annie explained. "You can probably tell which are which."

"They are all nice."

"I'm so glad to have your help," Annie said. "Thinking about working with you on these old pictures made me wonder—do you feel part of a generation—like a particular generation with an identity?"

"You mean like a Millennial or whatever?"

"Right."

"I guess not. No. I'm too old to be a Millennial. You are in the Sixties Generation, right?"

"Yes—we North Roaders are Baby Boomers. Shall we get going on the slide show?"

"Okay. Where will it begin?"

"North Road Farm, as a group house, started in the summer of 1973. The Watergate Hearings summer."

"What?"

"The Watergate Scandal? President Nixon?"

"Oh."

"It was a big deal at the time. We were young adults so everything seemed like a big deal to us. Anyway, they bought the farm that summer."

"Were you there?"

"No. Jack and I came the next spring."

"Do you have pictures from the beginning?"

"Happily, it turns out that Phil is one of those photo-album-making individuals." Annie took a black box off of a shelf, placed it on the work table, and lifted its lid, revealing the wine-colored front cover of an old fashioned photo album. Reverently Annie lifted it onto the table. The first picture showed four people in their early twenties. Behind them was a house that was missing much of its paint.

Jen recognized Phil, Elaine, and Jeff. "Who's that?" she asked, pointing to the woman next to Jeff. "The caption calls her Carol. Was she with Jeff?"

"I don't know much about her," Annie said. "She was Jeff's girlfriend when they moved in but she was gone by the time I got there."

"She was pretty."

Annie thought, *Especially next to Elaine.* She closed the album, untied its cord and gently lifted the front cover. Annie suggested that Jen place the photos on the scanner—"Your frame-shop work makes you qualified,"—while she managed the computer. There were four pictures on each album page. Annie scanned them one at a time along with the captions Phil had written in white ink. His photographs, Annie noticed, were long on people and short on everything else—an accurate reflection of his lifelong bent. He had pictures of each new resident and most of the visitors.

Holding a page she was about to place on the scanner, Jen said, "Phil was well organized."

"Anyone looking at this album could see we were not a hippie commune," Annie said. "Everything was under control."

"Does the album go until he sold the farm?"

"No. It ends when Paul is born. I'm guessing there is an album somewhere full of pictures of Paul."

Annie made notes of the captions. "Elaine and Jeff tearing off the old roof—August 8, 1973."

A bulldozer. "September 6—Digging the new septic system."

A tall teenager standing in front of the barn. "October 13—Welcome Rubble whose mother calls him Duane."

The boy painting the house. "He went right to work."

"November. We lost Carol but gained Karen and Boomer."

Rubble with seed catalogs. "February '74. Planning for planting."

Jeff getting into the truck with a lunch box. "March—Jeff starts a new job."

Rubble with a box of baby chicks. "April—Livestock arrives at North Road Farm."

A young woman wearing bib overalls. "May—Welcome Hoeth!"

"Here we are," Annie said. "June—Welcome Jack and Annie."

Jen said, "You are still just as gorgeous."

"You are sweet to say so, my dear. I'm vain only about my good posture. Some days that gets me by. From here on I have pictures, too. I've scanned the negatives. We'll have to figure out how to collate them."

Jen looked at a picture from that summer. "Who is that?" She read the caption. "Pamela." There stood a tall girl with black hair and piercing eyes, looking straight at the camera. "Who was she?"

"She was Bob's college girlfriend. She considered herself an anthropologist studying our tribe and its folkways but at the same time she was just playing at that, like it was her thing, you know, the theme of her persona. She caused a fair amount of trouble but she was always interesting." Annie did not tell Jen that the biggest explosion Pam had caused was when she rode off behind Boomer on his Harley, infuriating and humiliating Karen.

Although she believed that Jeff was Jen's father, Annie was not about to say so to Jen. Karen's disclosure about the encounter in the closet was safe with her, not only because it wasn't her place to discuss it, but also because Annie thought the story might not be true; Karen could have made it up. Even if Karen believed it, it might never have happened. On the other hand Annie wished Jen did have a nice father like Jeff. She wondered whether perhaps he could be led to a certain amount of paternal-ness to Jen without suspecting that he might actually be her father. But if Karen's story was accurate, wouldn't Jeff have considered that possibility? And been responsible? Of course he would have. Karen probably made it up.

They scanned a picture of Jack, in October, standing in front of the completed dome. During the fall it became the preferred place to listen to music and play cards. Jack and Annie spent some nights under it close in each other's arms in their double-sized sleeping bag.

Annie assigned the caption "Aftermath" to a photo dated November 1, 1974, showing the living room of the farmhouse. Stay-over guests were asleep on the sofa and the floor, surrounded by empty glasses, beer bottles, and ash trays loaded with cigarette butts.

"It must have been quite a party," Jen observed.

"It was," Annie confirmed.

The last picture showed Elaine, very pregnant, captioned, "Here comes Paul!"

Annie said, "Paul was born that December. Barb moved in not long afterward—early the next year."

"My dad died that February. Nobody rides motorcycles in February."

"He was a tough hombre," Annie said. "Also, he didn't have a car. Then at some point after that your mom left. I've forgotten—where did she go?"

"To my grandparents' in Worcester. She had me in Worcester."

"And that spring Jack and I moved out and before that Rubble and Hoeth had decamped—"

"Why did they leave?"

"As I recall her family had a farm in Minnesota or someplace and something happened—maybe her dad got sick—and the family needed her help. So off they went to a real farm—Hoeth and her strapping young recruit."

"The commune petered out. Why didn't more people move in?"

"I don't know. Times were changing or the idea wasn't new anymore. Maybe the people who gave us a look—there were always some of those, who needed a place to live—could tell that we were tired of finding consensus about everything. We'd had enough. We were ready for our own lives."

It took several hours to scan the photos in Phil's album. They worked for another hour to intermingle Annie's pictures with his. Finally Annie said, "That's okay for today, don't you think?"

"I could keep going if you want."

"I'm ready for a glass of wine. How about you?"

Jen was agreeable.

When they were settled in the living room, Annie said, "I got an amazing letter from Jeff yesterday. This goes back to the generation thing we were talking about when you first arrived. I'm going to scan Jeff's letter and send it to everyone who's coming to the reunion. You'll get it."

"What made it amazing?"

"Long-haired young Jeff moves to the farm and he meets the elderly neighbors who turn out to be Quakers. Our generation was busy holding revolutions and movements and whatnot but these old people had been there ahead of us. Besides, the Baby Boomers weren't very revolutionary, really."

"Why do you say that?"

"Because most of us were just like everybody else, trying to locate ourselves between the Freudian polarities—"

"What do you mean?"

"Freud said people need to love and to work and like other generations we tried to find both of those and balance our attention to each—except we made sure women had the same work options men had—honey what's wrong?"

Jen was crying. "I'm a flop in both departments."

"Oh, Jen—"

"And there aren't any other departments, are there?"

"As for work, you are a wonderful bird guide. I know that first hand. I bet you're equally wonderful in the frame shop."

"Thank you," Jen said.

"Did something from this afternoon upset you?"

"No, not from this afternoon. From yesterday."

"What was that?"

"Paul's girlfriend broke up with him and he invited me to take her place."

"Just like that?"

"Yeah, pretty much."

"I'm sorry."

"I don't even mind that part, I mean, I suppose it's kind of insulting but I really don't care especially because I could never go with him."

"No?"

"No. At least I'm really clear about that, but . . ."

Annie tried to see where she was going when she trailed off. "But it reminds you you don't have anybody else right now?"

"Right."

"Do you like guys?"

"I'm not gay or anything. Maybe there's just a piece missing. I thought Paul had it together but I guess we're both dysfunctional."

"Paul's dysfunctional?"

"He seems angry right now. I don't know whether that's cause or effect of his girlfriend moving out."

"But he thought you might step right in?"

"Because maybe I'm desperate—he could have thought that. But I'm not. I don't even want anybody all that much. Isn't that weird?"

While Annie tried to decide how to respond to that, Jack walked in. "Hello Jen, hello Annie." He noticed Jen's red eyes and his wife's distracted air and asked, "What's the matter?"

"Life's vicissitudes," Annie responded. "What if you don't want the person who wants you? What if that person is just reacting on a rebound? What if you are not sure about the line of work you have taken? The usual stuff."

"Oh, Christ," Jack said. "I think I'll have a drink. Anyone else?"

"We started without you." Annie brandished their wine bottle. When Jack had left the room she apologized if she had told Jack more than Jen wanted her to."

"That's okay," Jen said. "I trust him. I trust both of you."

Annie noticed that Jen's voice and facial expressions had returned to normal. "If you're feeling a little better I want to go upstairs for a few minutes."

"Sure that's fine."

"Supper's ready except for the grilling and that's Jack's responsibility so if you'll excuse me for a little while."

When Jack returned, he invited Jen to join him on the patio. Lighting the gas grill, Jack said, "It's funny that we've seen so little of you over all these years and then we traveled with you and appreciated your expertise and now here you are and we'll be with you again, before long, in Dutton."

"Yes."

Having closed the lid to allow the grill to heat up, Jack turned to look at her. Jen felt that his gaze was appraising. Wishing to remove his attention from her appearance, she said, "You have a bird-feeder." *That was lame*, she thought.

In response, Jack gave a lengthy description of food they offered, the behavior of the birds when he forgot to fill the feeder, the species they could count on, and the unusual bird visitors they had seen.

Jen half-listened. There stood a pleasant man, comfortable in his large man's body, with his strong face and steel-colored curls. The thought of how nice it would be to embrace a good-sized man, a man like Jack, took her by surprise. Recoiling in shame, she took half a step back.

Jack said, "This reunion is interesting to me. You're going, right?"

Jen nodded.

"I've never cared about school reunions, but this feels different. It stands for something. Like my dome!"

"It's still there good as new."

"Better!" Jack said. "When it was new it leaked. I could never get it sealed."

"Is it dry now?"

"Yeah. Jeff figured it out. He's really the man, the rock, isn't he?"

"I love Jeff." The wine had affected Jen's choice of words. Hearing herself, she added, "Barb too."

"They are great. They live the good life in God's country. They sell goat cheese, right?"

"Yes, they sell it but they also give a lot to food pantries."

"They can't market all they make?"

"It sure goes fast at harvest fairs. I would think they could sell it all. But they are Quakers . . ."

"Are they? I don't think that was true when Annie and I lived with them—I guess that came after. I went to a Quaker meeting once."

"Did you join?"

"No. I couldn't. I didn't feel good enough. I'm more worldly or selfish or whatever. Are you religious?"

"No. My mom's parents were Episcopalian but she let go all of that. Maybe I should check it out."

"Or maybe not. Time to put the meat on."

As Jack returned to the house Jen felt relieved to realize that the imagined embrace could have come from Jack as father rather than Jack as a lover. Her embarrassment dissipated. When Jack came back and asked what she did for fun, Jen mentioned her Earth Emigration planning. Because he showed interest, she added, "I know that would not be many people's idea of fun. I love to plan. Dependencies! Contingencies! I lay it all out on graph paper. Danger is coming. What is it? An asteroid? How long do we have? Or there's the mega-volcano scenario. In that one everything is dark and cold; nobody's growing any more crops, we're shut off from the sun—so off we go. Of course you could get more people to Mars or Venus than you could to an Earth-like planet but then you've got major problems with their environments. This is what I do in the evenings. While I watch a ballgame or listen to music."

"I guess it's kind of like planning for a birding trip," Jack said.

"Yes but with less supporting infrastructure," Jen resumed. "This life raft is going to be alone in a cold vacuum for a long long time. You have to think of everything. To learn how to figure it out, I take courses online."

"When do you do that?"

"Also while watching games on TV. I don't know why everybody doesn't do it. It's fun."

"Your hobbies are professional sports and preparing for the end of the world?"

"Not just professional—in fact I prefer college. I do like to have a game on, to keep me company." Jen was surprised that she had told Jack about her Earth Emigration Vehicle—she had never talked about it with anyone. She thought, *He seems interested.*

After her morning coffee had taken its full effect, but before the day was much worn, Annie sat down at her computer.

In general I hate long emails. I think this is the longest I ever sent, so, sorry. Blame yourselves—you got me thinking. This started out to be a mere cover note for an attachment—Jeff's beautiful remembrance of Sam and Rebecca Regal—but I feel stimulated by talking about North Road Farm and looking at pictures from our old days. The prospect of writing a piece about our generation has me excited. Maybe this is my warm-up.

I remember reading Tom Wolfe's *Electric Kool-aid Acid Test* and feeling the yen to be one of the Merry Pranksters—to be free and loose and creative and cool. There is a scene in that book when the Pranksters were on the East Coast and were invited to visit a Unitarian retreat. The Unitarians probably wanted to show their acceptance of youthful rebellion and to underscore their desire for social change and so forth, but the image I remember is the Prankster's disdain for the middle-aged Bermuda-shorts-wearing UUs who really didn't get it—and the subtext, as clear in my mind as anything from the book—*they are not cool like we are.* At the time, yes, I identified with the hip young people—but something caught on me. The Pranksters thought they were on a high plane, but in the end they were unable to build anything. Wolfe's book portrayed a tribe whose leader had charisma but lacked substance.

In contrast, North Road Farm was led by two guys who did have substance and did build something—a group that practiced feminism, or tried to, and that accepted individual differences in education, personality, interests, and so forth. Race, too, of course—but that was never tested. We were mostly privileged white young adults. Some of us (I mean you, Elaine) had a strong political interest and commitment that the rest of us learned from and were inspired and energized by. Others gained practical skills. Duane and Hoeth fenced the pasture, made compost, and became master gardeners.

Jeff built benches and shelves and fixed everything. Jack created his dome.

I would characterize myself as a partial lurker because although I was more than willing to pick beans and gather eggs and, sometimes, would pull weeds in the garden, I could never duplicate the intensity of your interests. I could see the beauty and appeal of each of them. My main endeavor was to finish my degree. I was fortunate that Jack identified North Road Farm as a place where he could try his hand at being a laid-back dome-building hippie man while I wrote my dissertation.

I can note that the subject of my dissertation was closely related to one piece of the complexity that was playing out at the farm and elsewhere in the world and forty years later it still is. This had to do with gender roles and stereotyping based on sexuality. The women's movement and gay rights—these are revolutionary changes that are not up for political debate anymore—they are off the table in the same way that in our lifetimes it has become socially unacceptable to sneer at an amputee as a cripple or to refer to African Americans as niggers. People are no longer allowed to spit a judgment of 'fag.'

Prejudice became linked to low intelligence; something to be mocked, derided, and rejected. Acceptance of others on their own terms was part of the summer of love, part of flower power—implied by *do your own thing*. This extension of the platform of social respect is a huge achievement. Don't you agree? In our country the metaphorical platform formerly accommodated a minority— high-status white men and women who corresponded to a narrow idea of normalcy. Everyone else stood lower—brown, black, foreign, handicapped, homosexual, homeless.

How and when was the platform extended? Who made room for the others? What softened people's hearts? Of course all hearts are not softened and there are plenty of individuals who would if they could push people who are not like them right off of the platform and laugh to see them land in mud. But, at least for now, those people lack social permission so to push. Somehow conditions were created in which we could be served by a wonderful black president with a funny name. Our generation was part of voting him in—no doubt about that. But before us came Sam and Rebecca—of our grandparent's generation, as committed to progressive values as anyone before or since. Doesn't the real credit go to them and their ilk?

I'm not sure how much we ought to pat ourselves on the back. I do think, though, that there is an *us*. Not everyone belongs to a generation with an identity. But we who were children in the 1950s, adolescents in the 1960s, and young adults in the '70s—we are a thing. We practiced what to do in case of nuclear war. We watched American officials—southern sheriffs and governors—openly defend racism. We went through the Cuban missile crisis and the Kennedy assassination and the War in Vietnam. We fell in love with rock and roll. We slept with boyfriends we weren't about to marry and took drugs for fun and declared ourselves liberated. Women's liberation, sexual liberation—liberated from what? From artificial restraints inherited from the past. We were liberated from having to follow forms we found hollow, meaningless, and distasteful. We stopped expecting ourselves to abide by conventions we hated and we also excused others from pretending allegiances they didn't feel.

We were not liberated from the work ethic or from desires to achieve distinction, to attract mates, and to live a life rich in experience. We were not liberated from the need to see our children, if we had them, grow up safe and sane.

I am so glad that Jeff and Barb have invited us back to the farm for this get-together. It will be great to see everyone. Thanks for sending me your pictures, and, in McBean's case, the movie, which we will show you, along with the slide show Jen and I have put together.

Until then, fondly,

Annie

The doubts of day-time and the doubts of night-time, the curious whether and how,
Whether that which appears so is so, or is it all flashes and specks?
–Walt Whitman

10

Jen accepted the call. "Hi Mom."

"Hi honey. Did you get Annie's and Jeff's letters?"

"Yes."

"I wanted to talk with you about them."

"Okay. What about them?"

"About your dad."

"They pretty much leave him out, don't they? Was he even mentioned at all?"

"There were mixed feelings about Boomer but—"

"Annie has the idea of a play about the farm. I can picture my dad being, like, the clown. Everyone else was so smart out there in the woods—all Henry David Thoreau—and he's, like, Buffalo Bill or something."

"Boomer brought that on himself I guess. But I wanted to mention that—"

"Everybody's so perfect except for him? I don't think so. Maybe they were snobs because they were better educated. Sorry—what do you want to mention?"

"Oh, well, so much happened back then even though it was just a few short years."

"You don't think you need to tell me about all the stuff you did, right? I probably don't even want to know most of it."

"Oh."

"The other people there thought more highly of him than you did."

"What?"

"Jeff's going to offer a special toast to him at the reunion. Because of how much help he was about practical things."

"I thought you said they ignored him."

"I forgot what Jeff had said. I was wrong."

"Okay. I better get off."

"Bye Mom."

"Bye honey."

Jen renewed her resolution to try to be more patient with her mother. At her drafting table she wrote,

I wish my mother wouldn't sound . . . like she does sometimes.

I wish I had a father.

I wish there was something I wanted to be so much I could put all my focus on becoming that.

I wish it didn't matter whether or not I was pretty.

I wish somebody needed me.

After Bob read Jeff's letter he sent him an email. *"I always wondered how you got to be a Quaker. I never knew it was because of the two seniors down the hill."*

Jeff replied, *"Rebecca and Sam were stars. They ought to have been famous. They would have hated that. They were great. Everyone ought to have known them, because they gave so much benefit."*

"You never know. Remember that guy I've always looked up to? Skeets McFarland? He's suing me."

"Ouch. Why?"

"He doesn't like my terms for selling Thundercloud. Somebody said Pamela's coming to the reunion."

"That was me. Carol might, too."

"Who's Carol?"

"My girlfriend when I first moved to the farm."

"Have you stayed in touch?"

"She posts in our alumni magazine."

"Do you know what's up with Pamela?"

"No."

"It would be strange to see her. We had animal chemistry."

"She was a piece of work."

"Like old times around the table," Karen said. "You sat here inside me and heard all the talk."

"I remember every word of it," Jen said. 'Like, wow. Far out, man. What a trip."

"It wasn't just hippie gas," Barb said. "Phil was already a good facilitator. We made decisions."

"Beans or lentils?—stuff like that," Karen said. "No smoking in here, right Barb?"

"No, but if the morning warms up we can move outside."

"Down to business," Karen said. "Make the plan. Jeff coming?"

Barb went to the stairs. "Jeff, you are needed. We're starting."

The four of them worked out a schedule for the weekend gathering. It would begin on Thursday—Duane and Hoeth would arrive that afternoon, having flown from Minneapolis to Hartford and rented a car. They were staying at a motel near the highway. The plan was to go out to dinner that night with them and anyone else who was on hand.

Friday would be farm day—goat milking, cheese making, bee-keeping, collaborative supper preparation, games in the evening.

Saturday Jeff would lead a backstage tour of the Greylock Music Center, with privileged seating for a rehearsal. Back at the farm was the actual party—costumes—after lengthy debate—would be optional. Annie's multimedia presentation would happen during cocktail hour, followed by a catered dinner and dancing in the barn. They decided to rent a heater and a portable toilet. They debated whether or not they needed a dance floor but deferred the decision.

Talk returned to the Saturday program. "Shouldn't Phil make a speech?" Jeff asked.

They decided that Jeff would quiet the crowd, focus attention, and introduce Phil, who would say anything he had to say then introduce Annie.

"Are we ready to talk menus?" Karen asked. "Can I make my guacamole?"

"Mom's guacamole has gotten better and better," Jen said.

"It's about using the right amount of lemon juice depending how ripe your avocados are," Karen said.

"More art than science," Jeff said, standing up. "I'll trust you guys for the menu and head out to my chores."

When he was gone Karen looked at Barb and said, "You're a lucky lady, kiddo."

Barb blushed.

"He's lucky, too," Jen said, "for having you."

"Okay," her mother said. "Can we move outside now?"

That morning, the Saturday of the weekend before the North Road Farm fortieth anniversary party, Bob wished smoking were a permissible activity. Not cigarettes. He had smoked a pipe when he was younger and he missed it—the appearance of the brier, its feel in his hand, the smell of the tobacco, the fussy process of lighting up, and the smoke itself. Tobacco smoking, though, was a thing of the past—unacceptable because of the deleterious health effects on the smoker and those around him. Bob couldn't remember the last time he saw someone light a pipe. He felt that he had been born to smoke—both his parents had—and he wished it had not become taboo.

Bob looked at the clock in his study, mildly resentful because that night the time would fall back one hour at the end of daylight savings time and this particular clock would have to be adjusted by hand. How anachronistic, to have to reset a clock. Bob decided to create a clock that corrected itself from the Internet, but that thought was followed by the realization that such clocks would already be on the market; that he had only to look for one. Would such a device also offer weather information? Would it access his online calendar?

Bob put his medication caddy onto his desk, took four plastic bottles of pills from a drawer, and distributed them into the compartments—fourteen daily doses. When each cell held four tablets, Bob closed the plastic lids. The finality of their snaps gave him the thought, *There go another two weeks of my life.* Had he spent his time well? How should he allocate his hours during the days he took these pills? As he anticipated withdrawal from Thundercloud, a new era approached. How, during the decade or two that remained to him, should he stave off entropy?

He wanted to be among what he considered to be a small number of people whose lifetime net against entropy was positive. By his estimate, only ten percent of his countrymen could claim to have produced more organization than they had consumed. He thought about this topic in relation to the boats he built and to himself. As soon as a boat was finished the forces of dissolution went to work on it. Dissolution—the fate of this body. Disintegration. Until then, create!

For the millionth time Bob wondered if his contributions amounted to the best he could do. He knew he was unusually intelligent, but had he made optimal choices about how to apply his talents? He had not been the right person in the right place at the right time to found Apple or Microsoft. He wished his legacy included a book. It was not too late for him to write a book but he thought that he was unlikely to do so. He felt that he had plenty to say but he did not feel that he had a book's worth to say about any one thing and even if he did he had no credentials to attract publishers or readers. He had capacities and insights but he did not have lengthy sermons to preach, stories to tell, or worlds to explore.

Bob had always been drawn to wood. Thinking *I have boats to build,* he went to the shop in his garage. The boat under construction occupied the farthest of the three bays. Bob's tools were in cabinets on the far wall. The workbench was along the back beneath a pair of windows overlooking the swimming pool, the yard, and the entropy-afflicted ruin of the miniature golf course his son had built fifteen years before. He flicked on an electric heater and turned to peer, through the small windows of the garage door, toward his quiet street. No one was going by—dog walkers kept their outings short on cold mornings and it was too early for the stroller-pushing young mothers and nannies.

A half-finished Adirondack guide boat lay on its scaffold, waiting for Bob to take the next steps toward its completion. He felt uninspired. In the past, when he was at his office feeling trapped in a meeting or performing drudgery at his desk, Bob had hungered for the phase of his life when the hours for making boats would not be scarce, stolen from work and family. When he could give the prime of his attention to wood and the tools for working it. He had always loved wood—to touch it, smell it, shape it, but this morning with the whole day before him and no competing claim on his attention he felt dull and unmotivated. This displeased him; the sale of Thundercloud would give him lots of mornings like this. Once the way was open for him to spend the prime hours of his day in the shop, would he stop wanting to be there? If he caved to Skeets or if the buyer withdrew he would lose face, money, and freedom—but the test of his motivation would be deferred.

The garage began to warm. Bob turned on the lights and the radio, which was tuned to Boston's classical station. He looked at the boat. When it was finished he planned to sell it on eBay, as he had each of his boats but the first, which was at Ruth's family's place on Stockbridge Bowl, where it served for fishing and stargazing and for taking visitors out on the water.

Ruth wanted to spend summers in Stockbridge after they retired, because the pond view was pretty and the Berkshires' summer culture attracted her. Bob had mixed feelings. That would take him away from his shop, his friends, and his habitual haunts. The Berkshire area was too hilly, at his age and weight, for his bike. If he was to be out there he would need a hobby. What if he built a boat designed for cooking and dining?

Bob sipped his coffee. The idea of a boat he could entertain on excited him. He pictured a mild evening on the Bowl, with swallows, a low table with low chairs, guests drinking and chatting—he pouring and grilling, the water calm as the day cooled and the sun dropped toward the horizon. Bob, the man who could serve supper on the boat he had created, felt the admiration of his guests and their sense of privilege to have been invited to join him for a memorable experience.

Bob laughed at the self-glorification of his fantasy but took pleasure in it all the same. He went to a well-lit area of his workbench that doubled as a drafting table, opened a drawer in a cabinet, removed a pad of paper, and lifted a pencil.

I firmly disbelieve, myself, that our human experience is the highest
form of experience extant in the universe. I believe rather that we
stand in much the same relation to the whole of the universe as our
canine and feline pets do to the whole of human life.

–William James

11

Watching Jack stake out locations for the dome's footings, Boomer had remarked, "We really ought to set this sucker below frost line."

This was not something that had been mentioned in the books about geodesic domes that Jack had read. "What? Below what?"

"The frost."

"How far down is that?"

"Some feet. I don't know. Three or four."

"Can't it just float on top?"

"Of the frost?"

"Yeah."

"No. Because the frost might heave it up on one side, see, but not on the other. You can't predict what frozen ground will do."

"Crap."

"That could fuck up your structure, see. Crack it right in half."

"Crap."

"Frost won't necessarily heave evenly, you know what I mean?"

"Christ. You think we have to dig down three feet with all these rocks?"

"How many footings have you got planned?"

"Eight. Maybe six would be enough."

"You don't have to necessarily go down the full distance because if you hit ledge you can stop."

"Ledge?"

"Yeah. Solid rock. Ledge. I don't know how far down you have to go here to hit it. Maybe the old man down the hill would know. Besides, maybe the kid will help you."

"Rubble?"

"Yeah. He digs. I can't because of my back."

"Rubble's fencing the pasture."

"And balling his chick."

Jack's dome construction went forward, but it progressed slowly. Annie liked the dome better while it was under construction than she did when it was eventually finished—the frame gave it that cool geodesic form but you could see the sky—the wonderful blue New England late summer sky, adorned, by afternoon, with puffs of white. Lying on her back inside the circle of the frame, Annie watched the clouds. Jack appeared with his water pipe. "Do you know what day this is?"

Annie did not.

"It's On the Road Day." Jack explained that sometime in August Kerouac had started across the country with Neal Cassidy, hitchhiking. "In the year we were born!" Jack and Phil and Rubble had agreed that since Kerouac had not named a particular date, they could choose one for themselves, and today seemed perfect so they were going to get stoned.

As he talked, he assembled the hookah he had built from a corncob pipe and a large glass flask he had liberated from a university laboratory. "We're going to toke up then build a fire and have a weenie roast in recognition of the holiday and in celebration and recognition of the *be there* principle. Care to join us?"

"Don't mind if I do."

In came Rubble—sometimes, now, they called him Duane, as his girlfriend preferred. His normally exuberant features were clouded. "Hoeth is going to keep working."

"Okay," Jack said.

"She says she'll try to do extra to keep us on schedule."

"What schedule?"

"Hoeth's gotta-be-ready-for-winter schedule. I'm down with it but today's a holiday."

"Right."

"It's against my religion to work on a holiday."

"Right on. Mine, too," Jack said, "now that you mention it. That might be my only religious principle."

A large black dog raced into the dome and greeted everyone with unselective love. A bearded, long-haired man followed the dog inside and looked around. "What holiday did I hear this was?"

"Seal. What brings you here?" Jack asked.

"Serendipity, my man. Serendipity. Nothing was happening in Northampton. I guess they don't know it's a holiday. What is it, anyway?" the man asked, sitting down next to Annie.

Suddenly feeling exposed and vulnerable, Annie sat up. "Jack has pronounced it Kerouac Day."

"Far out," Seal said. Looking at Annie, he asked, "What's your thing?"

"Nineteenth Century French literature," Annie replied. "What's yours?"

"Sex on acid. Interested? You are tough and the acid's on me."

"No!" Annie said.

"Jesus, Seal," Jack stammered, "Annie's my—Annie and I are—"

"I'm his girlfriend," Annie said, pointing at Jack.

"Okay, man, that's cool." Seal looked at Annie as he said to Jack, "Your old lady is tough, man. I don't blame you for not wanting to share."

"Yuck," Annie said. She stood up and moved over to Jack on the far side of the hookah from Seal. The dog, excited by her motion, thrust his nose into her crotch. "Jack!"

"Seal, call your dog," Jack said.

They went ahead and smoked—but the visitor, soon departed, had killed the holiday spirit. After the dog and his uncouth master were gone, Jack picked up a book. Annie returned to the place she had been before the others had arrived and stretched out on her back, looking up at the now-cloudless sky through the framework of the dome. The marijuana left her with a vague sexual desire. She considered suggesting to Jack that they adjourn to their bedroom— but the recollection of Seal and his dog chilled her—she recoiled from the obnoxious hippie's barefaced proposition. She knew that she was, although not classically pretty, attractive to men, but the self-assurance that made her sexy also put most men on their good behavior. Once in a while there was an exception—usually from a clueless individual like Seal. Considering what a jerk he had been, Annie felt sorry for his dog, who probably deserved a better companion.

Annie heard Duane and Hoeth, far across the pasture, call to each other. She wondered how long she and Jack would stay at the farm, and what the next phase of their lives would be. She examined her assumption that "they" was permanent. Maybe Jack would dump her. Maybe she'd move to France by herself. She wished Jack had been sterner with the creepy guy—then she accused herself of sexism.

Gradually Annie's arousal returned. She wondered what it would be like to have sex with a stranger—that was an experiment she had not tried. The idea was repellent, but also interesting—if the guy could look like, say, Paul Newman. A hawk coasted into her field of vision, its wings steady, riding an updraft over the farm, wheeling. Annie felt peaceful. With an actual man, there were always complications.

Annie wondered if she might someday have a child. Would she marry Jack? She didn't want to think about it. She tried to quiet her brain and watch the empty sky, divided as it was by the dome's framework into blue triangles. She hoped that the hawk would return.

"Hungry?"

Jack's voice startled her. "A little. Not too."

"I'm hungry. I could make sandwiches."

"Just a half for me."

Karen and her shopping cart were behind Barb, who also pushed a cart. "How many?" Karen asked.

Barb turned to Karen. "Huh?"

"How many people are coming?"

"The head count? Every meal is different. The peak is Saturday night when we could have thirty-eight but of course you never know for sure."

Jen trailed behind her mother, observing the huge store and its merchandise. Ordinarily she avoided such places but, having volunteered to help her mother and Barb shop for the reunion, there she was, shocked and repelled by the ambiance—the scale, lighting, decor, and acoustics. Looking for an upside, she watched for ideas that could serve her Earth Emigration project.

When the party supplies had been purchased Jen said goodbye and headed home. She regarded the upcoming event with uneven emotions. On the one hand, although she was basically a shy person, Jen enjoyed parties. She loved Barb and Jeff and they let her feel like one of the hosts. But it seemed inevitable that her mother would find ways of embarrassing her. If Paul had not tried to cast her in the role of girlfriend he might have offered a safe haven—but now that relationship was complicated. Then there was the prospect of hearing more about her father. Yes, she wanted to know as much about him as she could—but she realized, as she drove toward home, that she would be reminded of the vacancy in her life his death had created.

A text came from Joanie—Jen permitted herself to read short messages while driving. Joanie's text said that Tim was traveling, Miranda had an earache, the cat was throwing up, and she could use Jen's help. When she arrived, Jen parked by her cottage and walked to Joanie and Tim's house—the property's main residence.

"Thank God you're here. Want some wine?" Joanie muted the television and added "It's *Dancing with the Stars*—but I'd rather talk. Where were you?"

Jen explained that she had been in Dutton with her mother, getting ready for a party.

"I hadn't pictured her as the hostess type."

"She's helping Barb and Jeff. We're both helping Barb and Jeff. It's, like, a reunion."

"High school?"

"No—it was a commune that was at the farm where they live. It started forty years ago."

"Is it still going?"

"No, but the people are still around."

"Are you going?"

"I do plan to. I hope you weren't counting on me for anything here."

"Didn't this thing happen before you were born?"

"Yes. My mother was there and my dad, too, until he got killed."

"I wondered why you never mentioned him. What happened?"

"Motorcycle accident. I never knew him."

"That's sad. I'm sorry."

"How's Miranda?"

After they had ascertained that both the little girl and the cat were doing better and wine had been poured, the two women settled back into the living room.

"So you are going to this party," Joanie said.

"Yes."

"Won't it just be a bunch of old hippies? Why are you going?"

"They aren't hippies now. Except my mom—she sort of is. But really they are all just normal people."

"But way older than you."

"True, but Paul will be there. He was the other North Road Farm baby."

"North Road Farm? That's what it's called?"

"That's what we call it. Some people call it the mink farm because once someone raised minks there—"

"Minks can live around here?"

"Yes. There are lots of wild minks around here—"

"I thought they were from Australia or someplace."

"No, they live here—"

"What do they look like?"

"Brown. Long and skinny. Small. You see them near water."

"Any chance of meeting a guy at this reunion?"

"No."

"Are you sure it's worth your time?"

"There's going to be a tribute to my dad. I want to be there for that at least."

"He was a biker?"

"Yeah, I guess. And good at fixing things but Mom says he was messed up from Vietnam." Jen thought, *That's a nice excuse for being messed up because it's patriotic.* She pictured herself there on the couch talking with a person who thought minks lived in Australia.

"I knew a biker once. He was wild. I wouldn't go out with him; just knowing him was scary. You, though—you lead people into the jungle."

"The birding trips? They are pretty tame really."

"Snakes. Don't tell me they don't have snakes in those jungles."

"I guess there are some but I've never seen one."

"You don't see them until it's too late," Joanie said. The cat retched. "Your turn,"

Jen got up to take care of the cat.

I and mine do not convince by arguments, similes, rhymes;
We convince by our presence.

–Walt Whitman

12

Annie sat in the room that had been her bedroom when she lived at North Road Farm. Here she had written her dissertation. Now, looking out the window, she thought of Emma Bovary, then of herself when she had been a woman at the beginning of adulthood. She remembered being in that same spot in the sunlight, open to the idea of not marrying Jack, feeling programmed to marry and favorable to his candidacy as groom but inclined against the course of action that failed Flaubert's character. She thought of Emma's tortured ennui and her respectable husband who was easy to make happy but impossible to feel intrigued by. Flaubert had put the woman's fantasies into an idle body with a heart that cared for nothing but itself.

Unlike Emma, Annie engaged in meaningful work and appreciated the man who had eventually become her husband—but still she could identify with Emma's longing for romance, for conquest, and for edgy, interesting encounters. The question: is this all there is? ought by now to have been resolved, Annie thought. There should be no sense of disappointment and no appetite for novelty. She had always wondered whether, once she had lived, she would approve of the person she had turned out to be. Even now she could not decide whether she was generous or selfish.

An automobile entered Annie's field of view and parked near the house in the spot that had been reserved, in the old days, for the farm's pickup. A woman emerged from the car and looked around. Annie recognized her body language from McBean's movie—it was Hoeth. When a tall man appeared from the driver's side, Annie supposed he must be Duane—she had never seen him clean-shaven. His cheekbones caught the light. There they stood, fresh from Minnesota— Hoeth and her husband. Annie went out to greet them. Having had no contact with these two since they had left the farm thirty-eight years before, she couldn't decide whether to offer a handshake or an embrace.

Hoeth stepped toward Annie and said, "Were you a farmer here?"

"That's Annie," Duane said.

"And you must be Duane-formerly-known-as-Rubble," Annie replied.

"Just plain Duane," Hoeth corrected.

"Hello, Hoeth—it's nice to see you again." The women shook hands.

Annie turned as the tall man approached her. He took one of her shoulders in each hand and held her at a distance that allowed each of them to see the other's face. Annie's knees weakened.

He released her and said, "You look great."

Annie started to say, You do, too, but suppressed that. "Thank you! Welcome back to North Road Farm."

Hoeth looked at the field past the barn. "This place was in bad shape when we got here the first time."

"You did a lot of work while you were here," Annie said.

"Yes, things look better now. Duane's always been a good worker, I'll say that for him."

Duane had not taken his eyes off of Annie. "Still taking pictures?"

"Sometimes. I looked at some of you and Hoeth while I was putting together the slide show."

"When do we get to see it?"

"Saturday night. Where are you staying?"

"Motel 6. Hoeth likes to economize on lodgings."

"If I can't sleep in my own bed, I want to pay as little as possible for the use of one," Hoeth said. "Home is best. We don't travel much. A farm doesn't give vacations."

Annie pictured the two of them socializing after church, drinking coffee, eating cookies. "That's practical. We're less so; we're at an inn."

Duane said, "You lived here with a guy, right?"

Annie nodded.

"Are you still with him?"

"Yes. We married a few years after we left the farm and we're still together."

"Duane and I married as soon as we got home to Minnesota," Hoeth said. "I had three babies in five years and they all have kids of their own. Duane and I have five grandchildren. Duane is good with them. They're about all that can tear him away from his books."

Annie looked quizzically at Duane.

"I like to read," he admitted.

"He finished college at night. He majored in agriculture but somehow he caught the reading bug. TV's fine with me. There are plenty of good shows and you can learn a lot but Duane prefers his books."

"What are you reading now?" Annie asked.

"*Light in August.*"

"Are you enjoying it?"

"It's great. I'd already read *As I Laying Dying.* Should we go inside?"

Hoeth led the way to the kitchen door. "Where's your husband?" Hoeth asked. "Did you guys have kids? Is the house a different color? I think I liked it better the way it was."

"Jack's probably around at his dome," Annie responded, but Hoeth had gone through the front door and was talking to someone else. Annie looked up at Duane. "I'm happy to see you," she said, conscious of using a conventional phrase to express a surprisingly vivid feeling.

"It's nice to see you, too," he replied. "You've become even better looking. How did you do it?"

Because Duane was swept into Barb's welcoming embrace, Annie did not have to respond.

An hour earlier, when Jen had arrived at the farm, she had offered to help Barb in the dairy—but Barb gave her a different assignment. "I think Jack needs you. Jeff and I never got around to cleaning out the dome and Jack's trying to do it himself."

Jen found Jack putting a carton of North Road Farm labels into a garden cart. "May I help?"

Jack stood up and said, "An angel appears!" He explained his plan to remove the boxes stored in the dome to make it available for its original purposes, "Toking up and whatever." He laughed.

Jen felt herself drawn to him as she had at their house, when she had been caught off-guard by the attraction and had become ashamed of it. This time the feeling was less surprising. She wondered what Jack saw when he looked at her. She was the same age as the dome—old to young guys, but not compared to Jack. She had a good figure, she knew, and no gray in her hair. Jack had a smart, nice-looking wife—but maybe he was bored with her. She corrected herself: not bored with Annie but just with the same person he had spent all these decades with. Jen thought, *Perhaps, if we lived in a polygamous culture, Jack would choose Jen for a second wife. Maybe Annie wouldn't mind.*

As they loaded the garden cart and trundled it toward the barn, Jen imagined herself in the role of mistress. Would she accept money from a man? What a far-fetched thought! That would make her a whore. Couldn't she be a part-time second wife who kept a low profile? What would Joanie Eastman say if a married man was to spend time in the carriage house? Jen was shocked that she was having such thoughts. As the fantasy played out in her head, she supposed that she seemed distant and out of it—she could picture herself as distracted. Spaced out—that's the word her mother used when Jen seemed far away. *Come back to the moment,* was her mother's command. Jen forced herself to say something. "How does it feel to be back here?"

"It's funny because it seems like a long time ago and also not so long," Jack said. "When I built this dome I was an energetic young guy and usually I feel the same way—but now I'm toward the other end of being a grownup, like, maybe I've got plenty of good years left but maybe not; I mean you never know. Anyway, to your question, being here brings out the mixed-up-ness of the passage of time, you know what I mean?"

"Yes."

When the first load of boxes had been lifted to the loft Jen thought about that word. Loft. Aloft. Was there a verb *loft*? What did it mean? In the middle of trying to use it in a sentence Jen reminded herself to be in this moment and again she wanted for something to say. "I love the smell of this barn."

As he wheeled the empty cart back toward the dome, Jack said, "You know, I don't want to offend you or alarm you or anything but I guess it's only fair to let you know that ever since our time in Belize I have—I'm sorry if you see this as inappropriate—somewhat of a boy-girl feeling toward you."

Jen's heart stopped. Suddenly it seemed like a huge mistake to be alone with this man, a married man, Annie's husband! For once she was able to think quickly. "We have become friends. My friendship with the two of you means a lot to me."

"Annie thinks the world of you," Jack said, "and so do I. I'll never forgive myself for having been rude to you in Belize."

"You weren't rude. I was over-sensitive."

As they went into the dome he turned and offered a hug.

Jen gently pushed him away. "Jack. I can't do that."

"No," he said. "I'm sorry. Just put it down to more rudeness."

"I know you are just trying to be nice," she made an excuse for him. "But I can't."

Looking at the cardboard cartons and plastic storage boxes that remained to be cleared from the dome, Jack said, "Lots to do here. I appreciate your help." As he lifted a box onto the cart he added, "I wasn't just trying to be nice, though. Sorry."

Jen inhaled. While she helped to load the cart, she thought, *I have to help Barb in the house.* That's what part of her wanted her to say. She thought those words but did not speak them. The man's interest excited her. It also embarrassed her and she knew she mustn't encourage it—but she did not flee from it as quickly as she thought she should have.

When they had stacked the load in the loft Jack turned toward her. Jen retreated to the ladder and climbed down, holding tight to the side-rails, distrusting her legs. She lifted the handle of the pushcart and pushed it out of the barn and back to the dome. Jack followed, saying nothing. As they reloaded the cart, Jen avoided his eyes.

Returning to the barn, silently, they hoisted the cart to the loft, using the block and tackle, unloaded the boxes, lowered the empty cart back to the floor of the barn, then turned to each other. Jen shook her head, then stepped back and went down the ladder.

Back in the dome, Jack chatted, as though nothing was happening, about decorations and music and furniture. He was still running on about the playlist he would create when they were once again in the loft. This time Jen made sure not to hesitate while they were alone; she returned to the ladder immediately.

When the last load was on the cart, Jen said, "Jack, I want you to know that I like you—but you are married—and I also really like your wife." Before Jack could respond there was motion in the doorway. In came Annie followed by Hoeth and Duane.

Annie saw Jen's gaze swing from Jack to her. From behind she could read the tone of Jack's attention to the younger woman. And Jen's expression suggested having been walked in on. Annie could imagine Jack being interested in someone other than herself but she was surprised he would flirt with the shy, inarticulate, young-for-her-years Jen. She wondered if perhaps, because her response to Duane had been somewhat disloyal to Jack, she was now wishfully or guiltily projecting flirtation onto her husband.

Jack greeted the new arrivals with his typical warmth and Jen reverted to her usual expression of alert reserve.

As soon as she understood that Jack was preparing the dome for the party, Hoeth took charge. Hers was a hands-on style of command.

She dispatched her husband for a broom and dustpan and Jen for paper towels and glass cleaner. Annie and Jack assigned themselves to deal with the rug, which they rolled and carried to a weedy patch beside the barn. Annie noted the ease of their cooperation, after so many years of getting things done as a couple—they agreed without speaking on how to proceed. *This is marriage,* Annie thought. *This is what it's like to have a good partner. Knowing what to count on. Life is too short to replace this.* She felt a ripple of jealously, not of Jen exactly but of Jen's smooth young-woman skin.

Annie set off in search of a broom. Remembering the expression on Jen's face when she had entered the dome, Annie chuckled to herself. Girding for battle, she formed the intention of having sex that night with Jack. She wondered whether, during intercourse, she would think of Duane. She had not had an affair for thirty years, since she first taught graduate students. Those earnest students never challenged her nor made her laugh nor otherwise aroused her interest—but one student's husband was a tennis instructor and manager of a fitness club. The woman had invited Annie for dinner on a night when Jack was out of town. The handsome young husband had walked Annie to her car after supper as though to protect her from possible urban assailants but actually to ask if he could buy her a cup of coffee some time.

Knowing what he intended, she accepted the offer. At the ensuing meeting the man did an amusing job of mimicking his wife's classmates. He charmed Annie with droll, oblique flattery, and in a soft voice frankly acknowledged his desire to take off her clothes.

She answered that she would think about it.

They met a few times at a hotel for afternoon sex. Annie found their trysts exciting, at first, but her interest soon faded. The man did not find new ways to entertain her—and his wife, Annie's student, became visibly pregnant.

Even before she broke it off, Annie had framed her involvement with this man as an experiment, necessary professional experience, to teach her what adulterous sex would be like to anticipate, to take part in, and to remember. Extra-marital affairs played such a large part in literature that Annie thought she needed to include one in her life experience. Her fondness for her husband and her lover's wife's pregnancy made Annie feel guilty—but that, too, was part of the been-there she sought. When she withdrew, the man gave no sign of disappointment—Annie concluded that whatever questions he had brought to their affair had been answered. The affair ended quickly and painlessly. Since then, when other men had signaled a hopeful interest, Annie had discouraged them firmly and effectively.

Annie asked herself why she felt stirred by Duane. When she had known him as Rubble, he had seemed like a kid—a handsome teenager in a big strong body. No longer a kid, he had kept his other attributes. His wife had accused him of bookishness, which was no crime to Annie, especially when the supposed perpetrator had such square shoulders and an excellent jaw. In making her allegation, Hoeth had revealed one of her limitations, while her appearance and manner suggested other competitive disadvantages. Duane deserved better; Jack had grown a minor paunch and he had become predictable and here he was making eyes at a younger woman who, Annie thought, had emotional needs Jack was in no position to fulfill.

Annie returned to the rug with a broom and wielded it vigorously against accumulated dust, raising a cloud that blew into her husband's face. Annie pretended not to notice as Jack, blinking, retreated toward an edge of the widening cloud.

When they lugged the rug back into the dome, Duane was washing windows and Hoeth was plugging in a vacuum cleaner, which Jack volunteered to operate. Annie'd had enough of the dome. Before Hoeth could assign her a job Annie headed for the barn. The main floor, the principal party venue, was clean and empty, ready for the installation of a rented heater. The adjacent dairy—a modern concrete-floored structure annexed to the side of the old barn—was silent.

Looking up past the loft toward the rafters and the cupola, Annie thought the space could be called a nave. Sound seemed to be coming from under her feet. She located the stairs and went down to the barn's lowest level, where the goats lived when they weren't in the pasture. Jeff was shoveling dirty bedding into a trailer attached to his tractor.

"Hey," he said to Annie.

"The party hasn't started for you," Annie said. "May I help?"

"Nah—I've got these special goat-shit-proof boots. You can keep me company."

"Do you ever get tired of this? Are you planning to retire?"

"I guess I'll retire from Greylock some day. No hurry. I can't see shutting down the farm—ever, as long as we can get up in the morning. It's what we do—as they say. Retirement isn't a big topic around here. We're satisfied with our lives."

"You both look happy."

"Good." Jeff emptied his shovel. "How about you? Are you happy?"

"Yes. In my own way. If I'm not, I don't have any excuses. But there's always that thing Paul Simon said in a song."

"What's that?"

"'It is written in our hearts and our brains that life could be better than it is.'"

"Ugh," Jeff said, depositing another shovelful of bedding hay and goat manure onto the trailer. "Do you think it's true?"

"I'm afraid it's true for me but I have a theory as to why."

"What's that?"

"Because although you can have all the good things in life over time, it's impossible to have them all at once."

"Okay."

"And of course it's only human to think more about what you don't have at any given point than to loll around grinning with appreciation for what you do have."

"True."

"So I guess my way of feeling happy or my definition of it is to feel reasonably satisfied most of the time. I don't know that I'm wired to be, like, continuously joyous. Maybe some people are. I'm seldom as joyful as I should be."

"I could say the same."

"Your letter about Sam and Rebecca was wonderful. You write so well."

"Thank you, ma'am. High praise and all that."

"Does being a Quaker make you happier?"

"Hard to say because I've been one so long. How I would feel if I weren't one, I don't know." Jeff nodded across the aisle at a pen that contained goats. "Mostly, I'm like them—I just am."

Annie pointed to the mixture of waste on the trailer. "Do you have a big compost pile somewhere?"

"Yes. Do you remember how Hoeth loved compost?"

"No."

"Before she came, her guy, that guy—"

"Rubble. Duane."

"—he was getting into it—I remember him talking about the fertile potency of chicken shit—but it wasn't until she came that this farm got a serious composting program."

"They're here."

"Who are?"

"Duane and Hoeth."

"Are they? I better wrap this up and say hi."

"Do you want me to drive?" Ruth asked.

"No, I'll drive," Bob replied.

"Do you have your sunglasses?"

"Yes."

"Is the coffee maker off?"

"I think so. Shall we go back and check?"

"No. Did you bring a tie?"

"What?"

"Just kidding," Ruth smirked.

"Ha ha. I do have my wolf mask." Bob started the car. "Do you have a costume?"

"I'm going as a surgeon. I brought scrubs and tools. God, look at all the Halloween decorations. That's one noticeable change since we were young."

"The whole thing is about death, isn't it? It's the death holiday."

"Halloween? Lighten up. It's just fun. Costumes and candy. And pumpkins! Big and orange and locally-grown. Every season should have its fun. And now all the towns are doing the scarecrow thing."

Bob let it go—this was not an argument he needed to win. But to him it was the season of dying. The landscape had erupted in color but would soon fade to gray with cold weather close behind. Halloween might be fun and candy-filled for kids but it also represented darkness and decline.

This morning, though, the sun shone brightly, the trees and bushes glowed with color, and the roadside was at its most beautiful. Bob tried to feel cheerful.

Their destination, his brother's place in the Berkshire hill town of Dutton, lay a hundred miles to the west. Getting there required an hour and a half of high-speed driving on a busy superhighway, the Massachusetts Turnpike. Ruth used this time to catch up on professional reading. She had a stack of journals on her lap; as the car swung around the west-bound cloverleaf she opened one and left her husband to his thoughts. Not long before their exit, as they reached the Appalachian Trail overpass, Ruth said, "You've been doing that thing you do when you are nervous."

"What's that?"

"Pumping the accelerator. You haven't done that for a long time."

"Okay I'll stop."

"Are you worried about this weekend?"

"No, why should I be?"

"I don't know. Because of your old girlfriend or something?"

"Pamela? She probably won't show up. She was always unreliable. Maybe I'm jumpy about Skeets and Thundercloud."

"You have every right to be."

"There's a lot of money on the table."

"You've been looking forward to wrapping that up."

"Yes. God damn it."

"But there's nothing you can do about it this weekend. So you might as well forget about it."

"Right."

He agreed, in theory, but a worry could take possession of Bob. Even when it was unlikely that a worst-case scenario would actually come true, he could become convinced that humiliating events were about to occur—completely beyond his control. When he sensed himself becoming blanketed by anxiety, he performed a mental exercise. He folded the worry and stuffed it into a backpack, revealing a station of okay-ness and security it had hidden. Although his most energetic problems could escape from the pack and spread themselves again, they lacked their previous opacity—Bob could discern the less dismal place underneath. He said, "This weekend has its own issues."

"Such as?"

"We're in a funny position. We weren't really part of it. And there's always Elaine and her mouth. But even if everyone is polite and pleasant, peeking into the past forces the contrast between what you choose to remember with the way things actually were. That is stressful. And you are set up to confront what-ifs, like, maybe I should have been a first-grade teacher or more like my brother or something."

"You are too sensitive."

"Agreed. How many times have we come to that conclusion?"

"Many," Ruth said. "Try to relax."

Bob noticed how little had changed in the center of Dutton. Route numbers on aged signs marked the intersections. Across from the grassy plot called the Common, the general store looked the same as it had the first time he had seen it. Bob went in to buy beer. Craft labels from nearby breweries were on offer; that was an innovation. Another difference from the old days was that behind the register there were fewer cigarettes and more lottery tickets with their gaudy metallic graphics. Bob marveled all over again that the state's working people volunteered to pay extra taxes through this form of entertainment.

Bob bought a brown jug of Hill Country beer that he put into an insulated bag in his car. A few minutes later North Road's gravel rattled under the tires. They had left home early and arrived in time to have coffee in the house before the farm tour was scheduled to begin. As Annie filled Ruth's mug she asked, "Were you ever here in the seventies?"

Bob answered for her, "No—we started going out right after."

"I was here plenty of times in the seventies," Ruth said, contradicting her husband, "but that was when nobody lived here except Jeff and Barb."

"Right," Bob said. "I answered the question I thought Annie meant rather than what she literally said."

"Bad habit," Ruth said. "In my field that causes plenty of trouble. I train that out of young residents in their first rotation."

"I'd like to watch you do that," Annie said. "I could write about it."

"I hear you are writing about us and this weekend," Ruth said.

"I'm going to try. A short essay. I'm no playwright but wouldn't this be good material?"

"A play? About the farm?"

"About us and everything that was going on. Most of it could be set here in the kitchen."

"Where would you put the audience?"

"Downstage would be where the stove is. The audience would be out there." Pointing at the door to the yard Annie said, "That would be the upstage focus. That's where people entered and left the group. The door to the pantry would be stage right."

"Why did that matter?"

"It wasn't just a pantry," Jeff responded. "It's a room and guests slept there. So, hah, you never knew who might come out of that door. Like, for example, Pamela."

"Is she coming to the party?" Bob asked.

"Nobody's sure," Barb said. "Elaine told me maybe she'd bring her. Who knew they were still in touch?"

"My scenery ideas are so retro," Annie said. "An interior made of flats with doors—like a junior high production of *You Can't Take It with You*. But that's how I picture it. I wish we could show the cellar steps so we could watch Philip sneak down to fetch the forbidden baby formula."

"From the cellar?" Ruth looked puzzled. "Forbidden?"

Phil entered the kitchen at the sound of his name. "A small domestic dispute," he said. "Elaine's—one of Elaine's—political embargoes."

Bob rose to greet Phil, not because that formality was necessary or even appropriate, but because he was tired of sitting on the hard wooden bench. Others followed Bob's example; people stood up and some applauded the commune's pre-eminent founder, who had chaired the meetings and who had been vigilant about the group's well-being. Jeff's low-key style and quiet pragmatism had been valuable and steadying—but Phil had articulated North Road Farm's thoughts—he'd found phrases and descriptions that everyone could buy into. Phil had stayed at the center of the group while Jeff, with his job at the music center and his relationship with the neighbors down the hill, had points of contact elsewhere.

When Jack, Hoeth, and Duane crowded into the kitchen it attained a festive buzz. As the party got underway, Bob felt like a hanger-on. He was distracted by Skeets's betrayal and by the run-aground status of his Thundercloud exit plan. *It's going to be a long weekend,* he thought. He wondered why they had come—were they there out of duty to his brother? He watched his wife survey the happy gathering. Her expression was observant, calm, a bit world-weary. He wondered what she'd rather be doing.

One thing Bob was not worried about was that Pamela would make his wife uncomfortable. Ruth had no way of knowing how much he had enjoyed Pam's enthusiasm in bed—or wherever else she could shed her clothes. And Ruth was armored with what Bob called medical consciousness—a state of mind in which people's bodies were troublesome mechanisms whose inevitable breakdowns brought them under her care. As Bob saw it, at this stage of her life his wife was incapable of feeling threatened or defensive.

Bob envied Ruth's emotional serenity. She was a successful mom and a successful doctor. As far as he could tell she was free of sexual needs or interests. He, on the other hand, considered himself a normal guy with normal insecurities although he thought perhaps insecurity was a synonym for motivated. Bob still felt the need to prove himself; he could fear failure in any area of life. He believed that his head must be more uncomfortable, as a dwelling, than his wife's—but he suspected that his mind was more interesting and in certain respects more alive.

Bob's ruminations were interrupted by Elaine's arrival—she strode through the kitchen door carrying a large stainless steel bowl. "Potato salad!" she announced. "See how domestic I have become!" Other lunch food was brought from the refrigerator. Sandwiches and chips were assembled and consumed. When the potato salad was singled out for praise Elaine confessed that she had bought it at Whole Foods. Everyone laughed.

As soon as the group seemed restless Barb led them across the yard to an addition attached to the main floor of the barn. When she had resigned as administrator of the Arts Center to spend more time at the farm, Jeff built the dairy. Its three rooms had concrete floors and running water. The milk room opened to a fenced outdoor corridor where the nannies waited for their turn to be milked. The middle was a kitchen where Barb made cheese. The third room was Jeff's beekeeping space, dominated by his extractor—a big upright cylinder bolted to the floor.

Barb let guests choose an activity. They could make cheese with her, extract honey with Jeff, or take a nature walk with Jen. Bob decided to help with the honey; he'd done that before and enjoyed it. "May I uncap the cells?"

Jeff nodded, pointed to the stacks of sealed honeycombs, and asked Elaine, "Do you know about bees?"

"Not really," Elaine said.

"Maybe you'd like to hear my rap." No one objected, so Jeff explained that most species of bees do not live through the winter as a colony. At the end of one growing season they raise males and fertile females, who fly from the colony to mate. The males die but the females, the following spring, become queens of new colonies. "Honeybees," Jeff continued, "over-winter as a group; they keep their nest warm by metabolizing honey."

Elaine interrupted, "So the busy busy bees make honey how?"

Jeff held up a frame of honey comb. "In the spring these wax cells are empty. The bees fill them with nectar from flowers. They go from one flower to another until they have as much they can carry, haul it back to the hive—"

"And you take it!" Elaine crowed. "The perfect metaphor for imperialism! The bees don't need it—right? It's extra, it's surplus—"

With a resigned expression Jeff said, "I leave them enough for the winter—"

"So the colony's "surplus" is taken by the master while the bees do all the work!"

"Beekeepers work, too. You want a job, Elaine?"

She declared herself part of the imperialist system. Jeff set her to filling jars and applying North Road Farm labels. Bob uncapped the honey-filled frames. Philip ran the extractor and fed Jeff questions to enable him to complete the lecture Elaine had cut short.

Outside, Annie watched Jack walk off with Jen. *Could he think I wouldn't notice?* She decided that either Jack's feelings toward Jen were innocent or that he didn't care what Annie thought. She rejected the latter as implausible. Perhaps there was some other explanation.

Am I still attractive? She was not without information on this topic. Ever since she was a teenager Annie had kept a rough tally of the frequency of check-out looks she received from men. She first become aware of these glances as she approached puberty. At that age she had reacted with surprise, embarrassment, pleasure, and dismay. She had as yet no interest in boys or sex; attention from men seemed weird; she ought to be as irrelevant to them as they were to her. On the other hand, their interest was flattering. When Annie's chemistry changed she became intrigued with all aspects of courtship and mating. As her curves matured, the check-out rate grew steadily. The eyes of men accompanied her through the world—until the day she realized that young men had lost interest.

Thinking of her husband and Jen, Annie tried to take the male perspective. Few men would receive continuous feedback on their appearance—their total attractiveness was affected by their social and economic power. This was also true for women—but the attitudes men and women brought to courtship were asymmetrical, Annie believed, because women were mentally programmed to seek strength in a mate—accepting possible risks they incurred from that strength—whereas men were hard-wired by evolution to seek women who appeared fertile. Annie's silver hair counter-indicated fertility; she couldn't compete with Jen on that parameter. Would Jack actually wish to start a new family with a younger woman? Annie thought not. But he might like the excitement of having a girlfriend.

Annie marveled that she could perform this evaluation without feeling upset, as though some other marriage, some other woman, were involved. Why was she detached? She walked around the house. Returning to the barn, she looked into the shop, then climbed the ladder to the loft, breathing deeply, inhaling the scent of the hay. A narrow stairway climbed to the cupola. Someone was there already, sitting on the floor, in meditation. It was Duane. Embarrassed to have interrupted him, Annie turned her back to the man and looked out over the countryside at the autumn-colored oaks.

"Pretty," Duane remarked from behind her.

"I'll say," Annie replied. "I didn't expect to find you up here."

"I did not expect to be found here."

"Sorry."

"That's okay." After a pause he added, "I feel that I've come home."

"You do seem at home here." Listening to the breeze pass through the louvers and rustle the tops of the nearest trees, Annie wished she had made a more creative response.

After a long moment, Duane said, "Jack seems like a great guy. He always has seemed like a great guy."

"And Hoeth seems like as much of a go-getter as ever."

"That she is, that she is."

"Have you come to love Minnesota?"

"It's a good place. But one of our kids lives in New Mexico and two of them live back this way. Maybe we should move one place or the other. Maybe I should come back here."

Annie glanced at his beautiful smile, then started down the stairs. "That would be cool," she said, and she left him alone.

Bob watched with satisfaction as the hot blade slipped through the beeswax cells, revealing amber honey that would, in the extractor, be spun out of the comb. The room had been overheated to make the honey less viscous, so that it would flow more quickly. The room was too warm for Bob's flannel shirt—he decided to take it off and work in his tee-shirt. As he unfastened the top button a woman entered the honey room, embraced Elaine from behind, looked up at Bob, and said, "Hello stranger; how've you been?"

It was Pamela. She crossed the room and hugged Bob.

"I've been fine. How about you?"

"Me too. Did you know that Elaine and I are lovers? We have been, off and on, all these years. Never exactly a couple— " She let go of Bob, took half a step back, and looked into his face. "You know my wandering ways. Actually, maybe you don't—I don't remember wandering much when we were together. But since then, yes, on both sides of the aisle, as it were, a rolling stone, sexually speaking."

Although this was a startling quantity of disclosure so soon after a long separation, because it was true to the Pam he remembered, Bob took it in stride and merely observed, "Your life seems to have agreed with you."

"You got married, right?" Pam said. "And raised a family? I've kept an eye on you through Elaine. Did you know we were involved?"

"No."

"You started a company."

"I've been part of starting several companies and I'm trying to unload one right now."

"Is your wife here?"

"Ruth is in the next room learning how to make goat cheese."

"I can't wait to meet her. You look good. Balding, yes, but you can't help that, and anyway so what?"

"Excessive male hormones," Bob said.

"He could wear a rug," Elaine suggested.

"Is this a big secret that you hang out with Pam?" Bob asked Elaine. "Did Philip know all along?"

"Yes he did," Elaine said. "When I first seduced Pam she wasn't sure about sex with a woman so she wanted it to be a secret from everyone but Phil and we've just left it that way. Until now I guess. Pam seems to have emerged from our closet."

"We can all be honest here," Pam said. "Is that honey? It smells fabulous."

Bob unplugged the uncapping knife and led Pam and Elaine into the cheese room. Ruth, deeply engrossed in the delicate matter of curds and whey, not wishing to distract Barb and derail the cheese lesson, showed little interest in the newcomers, who soon left with Elaine. Bob stayed with Ruth, feigning interest in cheese-making as he absorbed the impact of this encounter with his old girlfriend. She seemed as lively as ever. She had apparently cut a wide swath. He counted himself lucky to have been with her for a time and lucky again to have married Ruth—a predictable, steady partner and a serious, committed mother to his children. And she earned a good income.

When Barb finished her demonstration, Hoeth said, "One of those ladies was Phil's wife, right? Who was the other one?"

"Elaine is Phil's ex-wife—they've been apart for a long time," Barb replied. "The other was Pamela, an old friend of Bob's. Do you remember Jeff's brother?"

Hoeth nodded toward Bob. "It's funny, not until this moment did I realize how glad I was to be away from Elaine. And was Pamela that voodoo freak who was here for a while?"

"Voodoo?" Ruth asked.

"Not really," Bob explained. "But she did take a participatory approach to her study of anthropology."

"She was too forward with everything, as I recall," Hoeth said. "I'm not sure I would have come if I'd known they would be here."

"I'm glad you did, though," Barb said. "It wouldn't have been much of a reunion without you two."

Assenting to the general need for her presence, Hoeth sniffed.

When Ruth asked Barb a cheese-related question, Bob left the dairy. In the barn he didn't see Pam or Elaine but saw Annie coming down the ladder from the loft. Watching her descend, Bob decided that he didn't want to be caught staring, so he looked toward the open doorway toward the house until Annie could turn and discover him.

"Duane is meditating in the cupola," she informed him.

They were glad to find each other because theirs was a safe friendship. Neither had figured in the emotional life of the other. There was no spark between Annie and Bob from either side and none between Ruth and Jack—Ruth had never been spark-prone. That couldn't be said for Jack, but he didn't find Ruth attractive.

Bob and Annie strolled onto the lawn to Adirondack chairs overlooking the pasture. The chairs reminded Bob of his shop. To advance the flow of amiable talk he launched into the topic of Adirondack guide boats. Annie showed just enough interest to keep him going. She found it relaxing to listen to an intelligent man expound on a subject she knew nothing about. She had enough general curiosity to be entertained and edified while another part of her brain reviewed images of Duane in the cupola and weighed the possibility that any sense she had of admiration returned from Duane was wishful thinking on her part. She must have tuned Bob out for a moment, because she was surprised to hear him say, "I go back to our conversation in the restaurant."

Having missed the context, Annie looked blank.

Phil appeared with a bottle of wine and two glasses. Bob said, "It's a little early for me—but why not?"

"It's a party," Annie said. "Okay—the restaurant. That's when I found out you were coming to this."

"And you asked my take on the commune and the counterculture which made me think of Pam whom I hadn't seen for so long and now here she is."

"How does that feel?"

"It's good to see her and so strange that she's Elaine's lover but mostly she seems like the exact same person I knew so long ago. I just didn't understand everything about her."

"She and Elaine are a couple?"

"In a part-time way. Whatever that means. That's one thing about our generation—the counterculture only went so far. Elaine and Pam stayed outside the mainstream but most of us picked up the middle class life style right where our parents left off. Except we have a car for every driver and do way more air travel and have hugely more access to information."

"I hope we have better taste than our parents," Annie said. She hadn't eaten much lunch—a little salad—so the alcohol affected her quickly. She heard the thoughtlessness of her remark, and recalled herself to her more usual style.

"And more sensitivity to the environment, we'd like to think," Bob said, "but I'm afraid we're just kidding ourselves."

"As we enjoy fresh produce, any vegetable, every fruit, twelve months of the year, we imagine that we are not materialistic."

"A tough claim to support," Bob said. "For us the word materialism is pejorative because it means valuing things for their own sake or as symbols of success or status. But the materialism of the world's peoples, at least as I see it, is the general appetite for food, shelter, and clothing and add to that health care and transportation which are material desires but they are not at the miserable level of craving designer this or brand-name that. Everyone wants a decent quality of life. Just think about our kids' generation . . ."

From inside her buzz Annie listened to Bob talk, enjoying his vocabulary, his pleasant voice, his seriousness about the topic. It occurred to her that alcohol increased his volubility; he became happy to hear himself declaim. She compared him to the other men at the farm. Bob lacked the animal appeal Annie felt from Duane, nor did he have Jeff's casual, good-guy manner, Phil's social radar, or Jack's self-effacing humor. She could see, but not particularly feel, the power of confidence and circumspection that enabled Bob to hold his own in his world of money, technology, and the arrogant super-smart. Taking himself seriously was, to Annie, Bob's chief appeal and chief drawback.

Annie realized she had stopped listening when Bob's mention of Jen caught her attention. "Do you think Boomer was really her father?" she blurted.

"Why do you say that?"

"He was a jerk and she lacks jerk characteristics."

"Ah."

"She's kind of nerdy. Not kind of—she's truly nerdy. You would never use that word to describe her mother."

"No."

Why had she gone down this road? Annie wondered. She loved the yellow light on the scarlet-clad oaks across the pasture. "I'm sorry. That was way random. Man, it's a nice day. This is great."

"It is beautiful here," Bob said, standing up.

Phil appeared with another bottle.

"I'd better hold off," Bob said, heading toward the house.

Phil sat down beside Annie, who held out her glass. "I'll just go ahead and get bombed."

"What have you been reading?" Phil asked.

"All kinds of stuff," Annie said. "*The New Yorker*. Books. There are far too many books, do you know that?"

"And more every day."

"How they scribble." Annie looked around. She wondered, briefly, where everyone was—but she didn't much care. She was happy sitting here with one man after another. Decent, intelligent men to whom she was not married.

A red-tailed hawk glided into view. Annoyed to see human beings, it cried, then wheeled over the pasture and disappeared above the trees.

Jen breaded the calamari. She thought that she and her mother would prepare the appetizer together—a demonstration for all to see of their companionability—but Karen kept stopping to tell Barb and Annie where she had bought the squid and how much she had paid for it and where she had made previous purchases, with comparisons of price to quality, as she slowly set up her electric fryer and filled it with oil. Jen had the calamari ready to cook and was cleaning up the counter before Karen gave any actual help with the breading. As she lowered the rubbery rings into the hot oil, Karen changed her topic to sauces. She hoped nobody would be disappointed but she had not brought any tartar—she preferred the red sauce people used for shrimp and she hoped that would be okay with everybody but if it wasn't she thought Barb probably had some mayonnaise and they could put in a little lemon juice and chop up a pickle.

"Shrimp cocktail will be fine," Annie said.

"Calamari's kind of a production," Karen said, "but I don't know of any better appetizer for fall, you know?"

"It will be much appreciated, " Barb assured her.

Jen arranged cooling racks, paper towels, and cookie sheets to drain the calamari as it came out of the fryer, then placed the crispy golden rings on a round tray with a bowl of sauce in the center. When the tray was full Karen donned a down vest Jeff kept on a peg, opened the door, picked up the food and said, "If they are doing dope this is going to blow their minds."

"They'll be glad to see you," Annie agreed. Karen pulled the door shut, and the kitchen became quieter.

Phil emerged from the back staircase. "Who will be glad to see whom?"

"Mom is rushing calamari to the starving refugees in the dome," said Jen, who had taken over the fryer. "We'll have some for here in a minute."

"I just heard the forecast," Phil said. "We might have a snowstorm tomorrow."

"A snowstorm? Really?" Barb stopped peeling potatoes.

"On Halloween?" Annie asked.

"That's what they said." Phil added, "That's going to really screw things up."

"If it happens," Annie said. "Sometimes everyone gets excited about storm forecasts and they don't come true."

Phil started putting bottles of spices and other ingredients onto an open stretch of counter. "It's time to make my marinade."

When all the calamari was cooked Jen took a plate into the living room, where people were watching television. "Seen anything about a snowstorm?" she asked.

"No," Hoeth replied. "It's supposed to snow?"

"That's what Philip heard."

Hoeth went to the kitchen. "Does anyone know where Duane is?" she asked.

"The people who aren't here are in the dome," Jen said.

Hoeth went out the door. Jen followed her, curious to get a look at the scene in the dome. Even though Paul hadn't arrived, leaving Jen the youngest by a generation, she felt comfortable. For one thing, she had, properly, rebuffed Jack's attentions—but she found them cheering all the same. And younger people would arrive tomorrow; Barb had assured her that the groups from Brattleboro and Northampton were bringing their kids and grand-kids. Jen was happy to be part of the make-ready crew, an insider.

It was black on the path to the far side of the barn; the night was cloudy; the sky was country dark. Jen thought about using the light on her phone but she was following Hoeth, who walked with steady confidence as though she feared no misstep on any farm anywhere. When they rounded the barn, the dome shed a dim glow through its windows. As Hoeth entered she said, firmly, "Duane."

Jen was unprepared for what she saw. Jack had preserved a collection of psychedelic posters with startling fluorescent colors and had lined the inside of the dome with them. They were brilliant under ultraviolet light. Because the black light was the only illumination, only the posters and white details of people's clothing were visible. There was a strong smell of marijuana and a thin haze of smoke.

"Hoeth." The tone of Duane's reply was too pleasant to sound mocking.

"We have to go."

"It's early. We haven't had supper."

"I don't mean back to the motel. I mean back home to our farm."

"Has something happened?"

"No. Yes. A snowstorm is coming."

"Here or there?"

"Here. We could be trapped. We need to get home."

To be heard over the Jefferson Airplane, this exchange had been at a high volume. Jack turned down the music.

"The farm will be fine," Duane said blandly.

"I'm uncomfortable."

"Can we talk about it later?"

"I'm going to check flights." Hoeth wheeled and left the dome.

Jen stepped in and said, "Amazing."

"That's just the way she is," Duane said.

"I mean the pictures. The day-glo. Amazing."

Jack said, "Shall we have another joint? Turn Jen on? . . . Hearing no objections, let the minutes show the motion carried unanimously." Laughing at his own joke, Jack struck a match, lit a marijuana cigarette, handed it to Karen, and turned the music back up.

Karen gave the joint to her daughter. "Here you go, baby girl, a little of the good stuff."

Jen thought, *In for a dime, in for a dollar,* and filled her lungs with the pungent smoke.

Karen looked at Duane. "I'd forgot how strong your wife comes on. I'm getting reminded."

Duane just smiled.

Jen noted his perfect teeth. She thought, *Mom likes him.*

As though to confirm Jen's surmise, Karen said, "Isn't she kind of a bitch?"

"Maybe it can seem that way sometimes," Duane said. "Her family has a hell of a farm, a beautiful farm, and she's inherited it, and it's a big responsibility."

"Does she own it or does it own her?"

Jen noted that her mother's remarks, though formulaic and ridden with clichés, frequently cut to the chase. Jen liked that.

"It owns her and me both I guess," Duane said. "Our kids dodged the trap, though. They're grown and gone."

Jen supposed that the oldest of them must be nearly her age. She wondered if Duane colored his hair. He had lots of it and most of it was brown.

"I don't mind her being strong-willed," Duane continued. "She always was. And I'm not jealous of her love for the farm. I get that."

"But?" Jack probed.

"Well, she's turned religious. And that would be okay, too, I guess, but the preacher, she can't shut up about the preacher; she quotes him to me all the time." That sentence hung in the air as Duane took his turn at the joint. Jen felt gratitude for the far-off clergyman who made this beautiful man resent his more-fortunate-than-she-deserved wife.

Exhaling as little as possible, Duane finished his complaint by gasping, "Tiresome."

Hoeth marched into the kitchen and asked to use a computer. Barb led her upstairs, leaving Annie and Phil alone in the room. "Annie, guess what?"

"What?"

"When you interviewed me about the farm it brought to mind the ideas I left in the orchard."

"Yes. Don't tell me they are still there?"

"No, probably not. I haven't looked. In the trees. But I did look in my old files and found them."

"I thought you left them in the hollow trees."

"I did. But I kept carbons. I found my carbon copies."

"I'd love to see them," Annie said.

"That could be arranged," Phil said.

Watching Phil concentrate on his cooking, Annie placed herself in space and time. She had a sense of being by herself—a peculiar English phrase, she reflected. There were people in the living room, out in the dome, and up in the office, and here in Barb's kitchen, Annie was conscious of the present as a unique moment in her life. She was surrounded, at a certain distance, by people she'd known a long time. The gathering included a nice man to flirt with and the amusing spectacle of her affable husband being friendly to a woman who might have been his daughter—this thought caught Annie up short. Might she *be* his daughter? It was easy to imagine some hour when Annie had been writing while Jack had puttered in his dome. Karen might have wandered in and, who knows? Why assume that Jack's lust was more selective than that of other men?

Annie laughed away that worry—it had happened in the closet—or with Boomer. But nothing was for certain. She supposed the actual impregnating sperm might have been Jack's as well as anybody's. Probably not Duane's—Hoeth had kept him on a short leash.

Annie observed how Barb organized her kitchen—her small shelf of cookbooks—not the culinary library that gathered greasy dust in some kitchens. The ample counters, well-lit—the arrangement far more satisfactory than in the seventies—two major upgrades had transformed the kitchen since then—and yet the basic look and layout had been preserved, along with the central table the old group had met around, and one of the benches Jeff had built when he had first moved in.

Annie pictured Barb as the spirit of the farm, hovering here in the kitchen and throughout the house, the barn, the yards, radiating a glow over her place that faded gradually into the surrounding town. The constellation of Barb's life—how well aligned—her house, her man, the farm, the Quaker meeting, her town—the orderly kitchen; the calm overall. Loudly enough to command Phil's attention, Annie said, "Under the barn, while Jeff cleaned the goat pens, we discussed happiness."

"What did you decide?" Phil didn't turn around.

"Jeff thinks he is as happy as a goat—he set the whole concept aside. I have my doubts, too. You're a professional: is happy just a word we use? Is there any there there?"

"What brings this to mind?"

"Barb."

"Do you think she's happy?"

"I'm noticing this great kitchen—functional and beautiful. And the overall feel of the farm—the health of the goats, the flavor of the cheese—it makes me think, a happy person must be at the heart of this. Because it makes you feel good to be here, you think the people behind it must feel good. Like, troubled people couldn't create this."

Barb came down the stairs. "That's nice to hear," she said. "How about you Annie? Are you happy?"

"Ugh. Being me, I have to parse the semantics. What do I mean by happy? Absence of pain happy? Short happy or long happy? Self-satisfied happy?"

Phil put down his knife and turned toward the women.

"Right now I'm definitely happy-short," Annie continued, "because it's fun to be here with you guys. Satisfied with my life happy? There I'd say, no complaints. Self-satisfied? Ugh again. I hope not—or, if on a good day I have some, I hope it doesn't show."

"Here's my professional opinion," Phil said. "You are both clinically happy."

"Maybe so," Annie said. "but I live every minute under the shadow of trouble ahead."

"What do you mean?" Barb asked.

"I don't know what or when or how," Annie said, "but everyone I love will die, including myself. So sooner or later, loss and grief will hit, again and again. The only way out would be to be the first to go, as though you wished the trouble and loss on the others. And you'd miss some fun. So what's the good of that?"

"Again I will speak as a professional, Phil said. "Time for a drink." He turned back to the counter. "I'll open a bottle as soon as these chickens are in their bath."

In the dome, Jen's cell phone rang. It was Paul. She watched herself slowly drag her finger across the screen to take the call, then looked at her mother and lifted the phone to her ear. She felt lazy and inert.

"I might not come," Paul said.

His voice drew Jen out of her intoxication.

"What's that music?" Paul asked.

"What is playing?" Jen asked the others, as she stood up.

"'Killing Me Softly,'" Jack answered. "Roberta Flack."

Jen left the dome and walked toward the barn. Paul said, "Killing me softly—that's what snowflakes would do, if I let them."

"That's a weird thought. Why would you not come?"

"Laura doesn't want to."

"I thought you were broken up."

"We are. But I had hopes."

"If you had hopes why did you say that stuff on our hike?"

"I didn't have hopes then. They came back to me afterward. But they turned out to have been irrational. She won't come and I don't want to come alone."

"But I'm here alone. I'm not crazy about it either. I might have stayed away myself if I knew you weren't coming."

"I might come. I'll see how I feel in the morning."

"Then why call me now?"

"Did you know it's supposed to snow tomorrow? On Halloween!"

"Yes. The forecast is available here."

"Maybe I'll go camping."

"Damn it Paul," Jen exploded, "I don't like being the only younger person here. I think you should drive out here right now."

"Sure, I can't wait—I'll be right there to get rejected again and cussed out and have a wonderful time."

The screen of Jen's phone said, *Call Ended.* She was in the dairy kitchen. Through the window she saw the light come on over the dome's door. People emerged and went toward the house. Jen sat by herself for a minute, feeling sad and empty, then followed the others. She entered the kitchen, where Hoeth and Duane were talking. Hoeth held two airline boarding passes she had printed in Barb's office. "We're all checked in," she told him. "I looked at the forecast and it's true, so we have to go home in the morning and I changed our flights and we're all set."

"Couldn't we have talked about it first?"

"You smell like marijuana."

"Everything in the dome smells like marijuana."

Jen passed the couple without looking at them but she lingered in the hall to eavesdrop.

"You didn't smoke it yourself, did you?"

"Sure I did."

"Therefore two more good reasons to leave in the morning are to get away from bad influences and we won't have to miss church."

Jen went into the living room and squeezed in on the sofa beside her mother.

"There you are, baby-cakes. We've been waiting for you."

"Why?" Jen did not welcome the collective attention of the older adults.

Before Karen could answer Jeff rapped on the gong he had bought, for this moment, at an antique store. Its rolling boom quieted the chatter and brought Duane and Hoeth in from the kitchen.

"North Road Farmers," Jeff said, "Barb and I welcome you. We're glad you are here and we hope you've had a good time so far. Everyone knows—but I want to acknowledge—that this whole thing would never have happened without Philip and Elaine."

"Whoo hoo!" Pamela shouted and clapped.

"I remember how impressed I was with Elaine's help replacing the roof when we first moved in."

Pamela cheered.

"I've had to do it by myself several times since then and she's been missed. We used to have a lot of hang-ups, you know, about guy's work and girl's work and Elaine blew that stuff out of the water in a hurry."

"Right on, Elaine," Pamela said.

"I was always a city mouse," Elaine said. "I don't know how you guys talked me into this."

"Which brings us back to the guy who has been our leader from the start," Jeff said, pointing to his friend. "Phil!"

"I wish Paul were here," Phil said. "But I'm so glad you are, Jen. And I'm glad your mom is, because she and your dad were founders here as much as anybody. The great sad thing at the farm was Boomer's death—we never got over that—it was our tragedy—and it's probably why we didn't last any longer than we did."

Inwardly Annie accused Phil of re-writing history for the occasion—then wondered if maybe he had always thought Boomer's death had doomed the group—then, finally, considered that it might be true.

"We were mostly student-types," Phil said. "We didn't want to go to Vietnam and nobody was going to make us. We wanted to think we held the moral high ground…"

"We did," Elaine injected.

"Maybe. We certainly liked to think so. We dodged the draft however we could—but Boomer in good faith served his country, not judging that he was wiser than America, not holding himself above it. He did what he saw as his duty and he paid a price."

"That's right," Karen said.

"And the people who loved him chipped in on that price, and those contributions from them continue today."

"That's right," Karen said. "Right on." She took Jen's hand.

Annie wondered how all this sounded to Jen. The fact that it was working for Karen might make it hard for Jen to take seriously. Maybe it seemed gratuitous and empty—or maybe it was just what she had hungered for. Watching Jen's placid face, Annie couldn't tell.

Phil went on to praise Boomer's mechanical genius—his ability to repair the tractor or at least to advise Jeff about how to repair it—his aside was a ray of true remembrance, thought Annie. Boomer would sometimes work hard—but never for long, she recalled. When he became impatient he used a line from a beer commercial: "It's Miller time!"

Closing his speech, Phil proposed a toast. "To Boomer Justice, to his life, his memory, and his family."

"We love you, Boomer," was Pamela's drunken pledge.

Elaine scowled at her, which caused her to lift her nose higher in the air.

"You fucking bitch," Karen said. "Just cram it."

Elaine said, "Karen and I have finally found something to agree on."

"That's one thing about this group," Pamela said. "You are narrow-minded prudes and you always were."

No one responded.

"It's not as though nobody else was ever friendly to someone else's guy." Pamela settled down in her chair and waited to hear if anyone would react to that observation.

"Or girl," Karen retorted.

Attempting to recover his original purpose, Phil said, "Okay, there are feelings around this stuff; nobody here is perfect; the point is, Boomer—he wasn't perfect either, but he was a good man and we were lucky to have him."

"I agree," Jeff said.

"I don't," Hoeth said.

Everyone looked at her.

"Judge not," warned Duane.

"Some behavior judges itself," Hoeth argued. "Like those needles he used."

"That was a symptom of what he suffered in the war." Phil said. "War's favorite injury."

"And you use drugs yourselves," Hoeth said. "Knock, knock, what's going on in the dome? Drugs. This was never a real farm—it was always just pretend. Duane and I are actual farmers doing actual life while you people show how useless you can be."

"What are you angry about?" Phil asked, trying, but failing, to sound non-professional.

"Good question," Hoeth replied. "Let's see, why am I disgusted? Is it because of what is going on now or what I recall from the seventies?"

"Hoeth and I see this differently," Duane said.

"I guess so," Hoeth said, "because only one of us is smelling like drugs."

"Chill out, Hoeth," Karen suggested.

"We'll be leaving in the morning. We have work to do on a farm that produces real food."

"Cheese and honey are real food," Duane observed.

"You know what I mean. Bees and goats are, let's face it, hobbies."

Annie watched Hoeth. This was supposed to have been an appreciative hour—ostensibly for Boomer, but actually to support Jen and Karen. Annie thought that the real appreciation should go to Phil—for how hard he had tried, in commune days and all his life, to help people feel good about themselves and each other. Usually Annie needed minutes or hours of reflection to crystallize her insights—re-playing the tapes, as she put it—but for once her line came quickly. "I'm hearing all this conflict and my first reaction is, 'Wait, this is a party, we're supposed to be having a good time' but then I'm realizing, no, this is what Philip created—he made it safe for us to yell at each other and be who we are. How often in life since North Road Farm have I or any of us found that?"

"Annie's right," Jeff said.

Tension broke and the room erupted into multiple small conversations. Annie looked at Duane, who wasn't listening or talking to anyone—he was in his own bubble, as he had been in the cupola, but now in the middle of the crowd, solid, self-contained, and handsome.

Jack took Annie's hand. "That was a good speech," he said. "You saved us. Or at least you saved the evening."

Annie squeezed Jack's fingers. She watched Elaine and Pamela. They were talking—each with a stern look on her face. They seemed to be the only people in the room who remained perturbed.

Phil stood up and came over. "I guess this meeting's adjourned."

"I guess it is." Jack headed for the kitchen.

"Thanks, Annie," Phil continued. "I've never had a more validating experience than hearing those words from you."

"Well-deserved," Annie said. "What should we do now?"

"Put the chicken in the oven. Be together, in love, hate, suspicion, rebellion, acquiescence. Our whole gamut. May I love you?"

Watching Jack leave the room, Annie sought a cautious response. "Philosophically we are as one."

"Thank you," Phil said. "You consented to my highest hope. I am on a roll."

Jen heard her mother begin an exchange with Hoeth. Apparently there was détente based on grudging respect for the other's plain speech—what Karen called being out front. Jen listened as they moved to neutral territory. Hoeth asked where Karen had been living and Karen explained that she had come back to Dutton from Worcester when Jen was a little girl because she liked it here. With civility established, Hoeth made a partial apology and said that a big part of the reason she had it in for Boomer was that he hadn't treated Karen well; Karen had deserved better. He had died and probably she should only speak well of the dead but, "I just remember how I felt at the time, when, he, you know, was rough with you."

Jen looked sharply at her mother.

Karen said, "He was gentle most of the time and sweet. Yes there were a few times he lost his temper but those were exceptions. I do wish he could have stayed away from the hard drugs—I think that was something either he picked up over in 'Nam or else after he got home to help him deal with his nightmares."

"Philip was right to point out his service," Hoeth said, "when others didn't want to go. I should be respectful of it."

"Thank you, Hoeth, that means a lot to me and Jen, it really does." Karen's eyes were moist. Jen knew that her mother could tear up for dramatic effect.

When the meeting dissolved, Ruth said to Bob, "Let's go make the salad." Happy to have something to do, they went to the kitchen. There had been times in their life together in which each had tried to manage the other—they were both eldest children and both bosses at work—but their urge to instruct had declined as they aged, and collaboration on the salad went smoothly.

Bob was relieved that he had been left out of the turmoil. It was unfair that Jeff had not been acknowledged and praised, but given his lack of narcissism, Bob doubted that his brother would care. He was sorry that the tribute to Boomer had been spoiled. Bob had known in advance that Boomer was to be praised for the benefit of Jen; he thought everyone had been warned not to contradict that theme—but

Hoeth had been out of that loop or didn't care and she and Elaine had created a social fiasco. Surely Phil had told Elaine of the group's intention. Bob reasoned that Elaine's resentment of men in general and macho-cyclists in particular—especially one who had attracted her girlfriend—was the dominant force. He thought, *She dislikes men and doesn't care that much for women.*

Ruth broke in on Bob's ruminations. "What did you notice about those little contretemps?"

"Maybe I could hire Elaine to deal with Skeets."

"Hoeth would be your better bet, would she not?"

"Skeets is East Coast slick. I need a big-city girl."

"You said she was from St. Louis."

"That's a city."

"Yes, but—"

"And that was a long time ago. She's been sharpening her wits and her tongue in New York and Cambridge for a few decades."

"This is only Friday. Things could keep getting worse."

"Nah," Bob said. "Tomorrow the rest of the outsiders will be here, a big crowd, and there'll be a different vibe." Jeff walked by. "Hey brother."

Jeff stopped. "Yo."

"They made it sound like Phil started this place by himself."

"He deserves that credit—he's the people person. I'm better off under the barn with the goats."

"Probably they are nicer to each other than we are," Ruth said.

"Yes. I'd go sit with them now but I've got to set up the living room." When the kitchen could not seat their company, Jeff and Barb converted the living room into a temporary banquet hall. The usual furniture was replaced by a large table Jeff had designed and built, which was stored, broken down, in the barn. Jeff asked Jen to help him bring in the table's components. As they walked across the yard, Jeff asked, "Have you heard from Paul?"

"He phoned a little while ago. He might not come."

"Why not?"

"His girlfriend isn't interested and he doesn't want to come without her."

"Ah. He's probably smart to do what she wants."

Jeff's remark disappointed Jen; she was surprised that he would offer an opinion about something he knew nothing about.

As they carried parts of the table toward the house, Jeff said, "Barb has really appreciated your help when you've been out here. She wishes you'd accept pay—and be around more."

"I couldn't take money for doing what's so much fun."

"Barb and I wonder if you'd ever think about becoming a partner."

"A partner?"

"Yes. In the North Road Farm business."

"Wow . . . "

"With a view to gradually taking it over."

Jen didn't say anything.

"We both know you'd be great at it."

"Wow."

"If you could think about living this far from the city."

"I'm really flattered."

"I hope you'll think about it. It would be a big help to Barb."

"You're not just trying to make me feel better?"

"No. Better about what?"

"The thing about my dad."

"No. Barb and I talked about this and I agreed to mention it. But, criminy, you never know what's going to come out of people's mouths, do you?"

"No."

"Was that painful to you in there? I guess it must have been. I'm sorry."

"It's okay."

Jen and Jeff assembled the table and unrolled a red checked oil cloth down the length of its plywood surface. As others brought in plates and silverware, Jen thought, *I'll light the candles.*

God changes his appearance every second. Blessed is the man who
can recognize him in all his disguises.

–Nikos Kazantzakis, Zorba the Greek

13

After supper, back at the inn, Annie closed the bathroom door as she undressed. She watched herself in the mirror, to see how she would look to a new lover. She thought she was a little too fat—but because she believed that almost everyone almost always thought that, she guessed that her figure was probably okay. She wished her breasts had not sagged even a little, but given her age and the unremitting pull of gravity she supposed they remained as attractive as could be expected. Annie dropped her flannel nightgown over her head and opened the door.

Jack was in bed on his back. Without opening his eyes, he asked, "Did you enjoy the day?"

"I did. You?"

"Sure."

"What stands out?"

"My old poster collection had its hour of glory. In my dome."

"Your young girlfriend was impressed?"

"Jen? There does seem to be a vacancy for a boyfriend but what can an old married man give her that would be of use?"

"Good question."

"What was big for you today?"

"How nice Duane turned out to be."

"Oh. Too bad."

"What's too bad?"

"Too bad he's leaving."

"Yes. Well, I've still got you."

"Unless I go for Jen."

"She's kind of sexy."

"It's not as though she's pretty."

"Don't you think her lips are sexy?"

"Sure—but her mouth is too wide for her face."

"You don't like to kiss anyway. But maybe that mouth, you would. And she has smooth young skin."

"Your skin's still smooth."

"Between my wrinkles."

Jack sighed. "I suppose you'd love it if I ran off with her. Then you could have new adventures without needing to dump me."

"I could follow Duane to Minnesota and take out Hoeth."

"She might be too much for you. I see her on a big tractor, with a shotgun, chasing you across a mile-wide field. You go down."

"I would employ stealth and treachery."

"Make sure to keep the element of surprise on your side. Don't let her determination become engaged or you are cooked."

"I am sad that they are leaving. I wish I'd shown my pictures tonight so they could have seen them."

"You could put them online."

"Not the same." Annie offered her husband their ritual before-sleep kiss, which he returned. Forgetting her intention to seduce him, she rolled onto her side and fell asleep.

In the morning Jack elected to take a break from the reunion. He decided to stay at the inn and watch old movies—his favorite form of relaxation.

Annie stopped at a bakery for scones. When she arrived at the farmhouse, Pamela was just driving away.

Elaine stood in the yard. Pointing at the car rumbling down the narrow road she said, "Pam's mad."

"Oh dear." Annie's sympathy sounded faint.

"I don't blame her really. I probably am a controlling bitch. But it's not my fault she's bipolar. That's my amateur diagnosis. We'll see what Philip says when I describe her behavior."

Coffee was being poured and Annie was putting her scones onto a plate when another car pulled into the yard. It was Duane.

As he came in the kitchen door, Elaine said, "You aren't in Minnesota."

"Not even on an airplane," Annie added.

"Nah. I wasn't ready to go," Duane said. "Too bad after all those fond farewells last night—wasted. Hoeth can take them home with her."

"Good. You'll get to see the slide show," Annie said. She trusted her natural reserve to disguise how pleased she was.

"The schedule said Jeff's giving us a tour of Greylock this morning. I was afraid I'd missed it. No snow yet. When do we head out?"

The tour left an hour later, with all of the participants in one car. Bob was at the wheel. Annie was in the back between Duane and Jeff, wishing the ride could go on forever.

Elaine was in front in the passenger seat. "Why did your wife decide not to come?" she asked Bob.

This question intruded on Bob's train of thought. He had been hearing, in his memory, his dermatologist telling him that, no, the itchy place on the back of his hand did not mean that he had fatal skin cancer. Bob recalled the pity and condescension in his tone, addressed to the hypochondria of a man whose skin needed a little moisturizer. This fantasy had been generated by Bob supposing that the itchy place was a symptom of cancer that would turn out to be fatal because he had scratched it sending tumorlettes through his bloodstream to (the dreadful verb) metastasize hither and yon in his body—his life expectancy was months—but a second voice in his brain had been ridiculing his fretfulness. Elaine penetrated his fog. "Ruth? I'm not sure. Probably she needed to work."

"You sound kind of vague about it," Elaine said.

"That would be it. She would have had to work."

"Did you check with her? Maybe she wanted to come and didn't know we were leaving."

Bob was, for a moment, troubled by this possibility until he remembered that someone had invented mobile phones, and he had one. "She could call. I think she told me she was staying put." To change the subject he added a question: "What's been on your mind lately, Elaine?"

"Our sham democracy."

"We've got this terrible congress."

"Dreadful."

"It's amazing that low and middle income people vote for these Republicans."

"It's not amazing," she corrected him. "It's the money."

"And Supreme Court conservatives overturning campaign finance reform . . . "

"Money corrupts the whole system." Her voice was rising. "We claim to be a democracy but we really are not."

"I kind of have to agree with you."

"That's funny because haven't you, by your own choice, spent your life in the money-making system we're talking about?"

The back seat fell silent. "I've helped start companies," Bob replied.

"Didn't you say that you are trying right this minute to sell a company?"

"Yes, that's so."

"I guess some big corporation will buy it and all those jobs will disappear but you will put the money into your pocket and go whistling down the street."

"If the company sells, which is complicated right now and I'm getting sued over, most of the money will go to the venture capital firms that invest in start-ups. And most employees will remain in place."

"I know your jargon," Elaine said. "You call them Vee-Cees, don't you? And you talk about a space, meaning what you sell, and getting rounds of funding. I hear it all and it makes me sick."

"That's some of our lingo, yes, but I don't know why it sickens you."

"You think it has nothing to do with income disparity in the country?"

"I think it has to do with having a healthy economy."

"Healthy for the top few percent and sick for everyone below."

"I'm sure you could paint a picture that ostensibly shows that—but someone else could paint a picture of how it keeps unemployment low, in relative terms, and gives a lot of people comfortable incomes."

"While a few people get stinking rich and a big group falls into minimum wage service jobs because their decent working class jobs don't exist anymore or at least they don't exist here because multi-national corporations have shipped them overseas."

"The global economy creates employment in countries other than the United States, which seems like a good thing." Bob sounded only slightly defensive.

"Those countries don't have organized labor and they don't protect their environments. Not that I'm saying we do a good job of protecting our environment but they do even worse."

"I grant you that the developing countries need to progress in those areas but I think if we looked into it we would find that progress is the result of economic activity—one of many desirable results including improvements in education, health, the arts, the status of women—all following behind, not coming in advance of, economic activity."

"Oh you have it all mapped out—your self-justification."

Bob laughed. "I wouldn't claim my thought processes are more independent of my self interest than anyone else's."

"That's honest."

"I can tell you, though, that I do my best to let thought guide my choices as much as I can, and I don't think anyone can do more than that."

"You have a line of patter for everything, don't you?"

"I know there are other opinions and ways of looking at this stuff but we all have to use our own best information and observations—"

"That's my point. What you call information is controlled by the media. Which is big corporations."

"You might have been able to say that before cable television and the Internet but I don't know how you can say it now. The days in which there were only a few television networks and news services are gone. If you want to you can watch Al Jazeera or anything else. You can read anybody's blog."

"You can, but people are brainwashed anyway. How can you deny that the system has them where it wants them? Why else would they eat that garbage at McDonald's?"

"I'll tell you why—because they like the way it tastes, the quantity they get for their dollar, and the reliability of the brand."

"Intellectual justification from a career capitalist. It's because even little kids are brainwashed to think that they're supposed to like that stuff. The thing is, Bob, that you Democrat businessmen—you are a Democrat aren't you?"

"Yes I am."

"Turn left at the light," Jeff said from the back seat.

"You Democrat businessmen sanitize—you spray air freshener over a stinking mess. We'll never have social justice in this country with you in the way, protecting the out-and-out pigs—the frankly out-and-out greedy ones—with your false rhetoric about gradual progress. Which I'm afraid you actually believe and that's why you're dangerous."

"Second exit from the rotary," Jeff said.

Bob followed Jeff's direction, then said, "You admit, though, there has been progress."

"No! No. I don't see any progress. We have hunger, suffering, crappy schools and childcare and healthcare, violent racial prejudice—lynching is what the police behavior amounts to— epidemic domestic abuse, poverty's getting worse—how can you even use the word 'progress'?"

"Because a lot of behavior that used to be okay is not okay anymore. To take domestic abuse, for example, there wasn't even a name for it; violence in the home was not to be spoken of. We haven't eliminated it but it is illegal, condemned, and we are trying to deal with it. The response is messy, complicated, and incomplete—but that's what incremental progress always looks like. In race relations, let's see, hmmm, we have for our president and commander in chief an African-American. Whereas the country formerly authorized and defended chattel slavery. As for women, we're headed for Greylock—when Jeff started there, how many women played in the orchestra?"

"Maybe two," Jeff said.

"And a few years earlier it would have been zero and now the orchestras are full of women and so are medical schools and law schools."

"And when they get out they still don't make equal pay with men," Elaine said.

"Turn left into that gate and park," Jeff said.

Sliding across the back seat, emerging into the cold air under the gray sky, Annie watched Bob and Elaine follow Jeff toward the compound's staff gate. Elaine was still talking, but there was something about her posture that suggested that the argument was over.

"How would you score that?" Duane asked Annie.

"What?"

"As a fight. I didn't see a knockout."

"No knockout. Points?"

"I'd give it to Bob although Elaine's sure a crowd-pleaser and we'd have to dock Bob some for smugness."

"That sounds about right." Annie had not followed all of the front-seat dialogue. She had savored her time between two men she found thoroughly likeable and attractive.

They traipsed behind Jeff through chilly air damp with oncoming snow. He gave them a back-stage look at the two main performance spaces. "Where's your office?" someone asked, which resulted in a visit to the facilities compound, in a corner of the property screened by hemlocks. Although invisible to concert-goers, Jeff's office was sited to give him a view of Mount Greylock and the intervening landscape. Annie mentally put Duane into Jeff's job and pictured having a long conversation with him here, on a day when no one else was around. They would discuss books, and the teaching of writing, and make affectionate fun of the quirks of their friends. He might ask her to misbehave.

When it was time to take seats for the rehearsal, Jeff led them back to the indoor performance space. Annie and Duane fell behind the others.

"Was Hoeth angry that you didn't go home with her?"

"Yes."

"Are you having second thoughts?"

"I'm happy to be right where I am."

"The two of you seem very different," Annie ventured.

"That's been true for a long time."

"Is this the first time you've pushed back?"

"I declared the Rights of Man some time ago but I went along with the overall plan of being farmers together and raising our kids while I gave myself an education."

"Did you take courses?"

"A few, but mostly I read. And watched educational television and now that I'm back among the North Road Farmers it feels like it was a mistake ever to have gone away."

"Really? Four decades in the wrong place?"

"Who knows? I love my kids. But Annie I'm just so glad to see you and Jack and the others."

"You fit in just as well as you did when we called you Rubble. You wear your decades well."

"As do you, may I say."

Annie looked at him. "Haven't you been awfully isolated?"

"I never felt isolated. Our children saved me."

"How'd they do that?"

"They admitted me to friendship. We talked the whole time they were growing up, and I drove them wherever, and we had their friends to our place. The kids were plugged into the big world—especially the digital world. They weren't interested in commodity prices or who would be the new church minister—so all I had to do was listen to them and watch over their shoulders. And besides, the hippest media is online so, no, I didn't feel isolated. There are plenty of smart liberal-minded people out there, you know—that might be easy to forget here where the East Coast intelligentsia swim in their true-blue waters."

They filed into the concert building—not the large pavilion used in the summer, but a smaller space that could be closed and heated. By some mixture of chance and intention, Duane and Annie sat in the row behind their friends. Annie was amused to see the musicians in casual attire—both they and their audience wore Saturday clothes. As the orchestra tuned, Duane talked about his children, their interests, girlfriends and boyfriends, their educations and budding careers. Annie watched the room as she listened. At some signal—she couldn't tell what it was—the audience quieted. The conductor stepped onto the podium and addressed the orchestra briefly, inaudibly to the audience. The players lifted their instruments, and music filled the hall.

Annie glanced at Duane. He had produced a small spiral-bound notepad and a pen. He flipped pages until he reached a blank. When he began to write, Annie watched his hand. He showed her what he had written: *Jack is lucky to have you.*

Although Annie did her best to appear to shift her attention to the music, she noticed that Duane left the pad within her reach. After a minute she picked it up and wrote, *When will you go home?*

Uncertain. Leaning toward "never."

?

Hoeth and I have been finished a long while. When Annie had read that, he added, *Ten-plus years co-farmers, co-parents.*

A minute later he added, *I had a girlfriend until a year ago.*

?

Died. Cancer.

Sorry.

Thanks.

Onstage, cellos and violas throbbed beneath violins and woodwinds. Annie placed her hand over Duane's, as if to comfort him for his loss.

Duane took his windbreaker from the back of his seat and laid it over their adjacent arms. In the privacy underneath, he took Annie's hand and held it for the rest of the rehearsal. To Annie, the music sounded great.

Room service provided Jack with a carafe of coffee, which he planned to sip in bed while watching *A Christmas in Connecticut*—one of his year-end rituals. Halloween, the holiday season's advance event, was earlier than he usually watched this movie but there was snow in the forecast—that was early, too. It wouldn't be the same without Annie, who could usually be persuaded to watch it with him, although for her its charm had worn thin. But, somehow, perhaps because of the inn's rural setting, he found himself in the mood.

Jack tried to stream the film through the hotel's Wi-Fi. At first it worked, but then the picture flickered, broke up, and froze. It resumed, but not for long. When the interruption had repeated several times, Jack gave up. Whether the inn had insufficient bandwidth or the router was too far from his room, or for some other cause, he was not going to see the movie. He checked his email. Nothing there. He stared vacantly out the window. The urge came upon him to be in his dome when the snow started. He dressed and had himself driven to the farm.

It seemed that no one was around. The dome was cold. Flat gray light penetrated the plexiglas triangles. For a moment Jack wished he had gone with the others to Greylock, but then he saw Barb and Jen outside the barn, busy with the goats, which made him glad to be where he was. He plugged in an electric radiator, turned it on high, and waited to see whether its load would throw a circuit breaker. It did not. To limit the current being pulled through the extension cord from the barn, Jack left the light off—but because his new plan for the morning included music, he turned on the amplifier and launched a Fleetwood Mac album on his iPod.

Jack's intention was to lie back in one of the bean-bag chairs, listen to music, and watch for the first snowflake. He tried to relax. But he had drunk all the coffee the inn had brought to his room; he was fidgety. He decided some marijuana would balance the caffeine. He went to the house for a pitcher of water, then to his car, where he removed a wooden box. Jack had made that box himself, at the farm, in Jeff's shop in the barn. It was a custom-fitted case for the water pipe he had put together from glassware, stoppers, and tubing purloined from a college laboratory.

Back in the dome, Jack took out the hookah's parts, starting with the large Erlenmeyer flask, which he filled with water. He connected the bowl of a corncob pipe to the glass tubing which he had bent, using a Bunsen burner, at a time when he still remembered how to do such things. As he paused to admire his handiwork, Jen came into the dome.

"What's that?" she asked.

"My water pipe," Jack said. He put the end of the tube into his mouth and sucked, drawing bubbles through the water. Looking at Jen, Jack said, "Annie asked if I'm falling in love with you."

"Why does she want to know that?"

"She thinks it concerns her, I guess. The busybody."

"It's funny to think of anything like that."

"What kind of funny?"

"Funny ha ha mostly. A little funny interesting. And totally out of the question."

After he had digested the complexity of her response, Jack said, "I shall draw the following conventional observation: 'Why can't a man and a woman be friends without exciting comment?'"

"If circumstances were different," Jen said, "well . . . never mind."

"Does that mean you do have a little crush on me? Because, full disclosure, I certainly have one on you, right across the difference in age, dirty old man that I am, but that doesn't mean I don't love my wife, who so it turns out was quite impressed by Bubble or Duane or whatever we're supposed to call him now."

"Duane is quite the hunk."

"Lucky for me he's gone."

"He isn't."

"Isn't what?"

"Gone."

"I thought his wife took him home."

"He slipped the leash. She went. He stayed."

"Where is he?"

"With your wife—and the others—over at Greylock."

Jack laughed.

Jen laughed, too.

Karen came in the door. "You've got it warm in here." She looked at the water pipe. "Are we going to toke up?"

Jack made a noncommittal gesture.

"I thought I'd better come over and chaperon you two," Karen said, in her cigarette-flattened wheeze.

"Butt out, Mom," Jen said.

"I was just kidding," Karen said. Leaning toward the door, she added, "If you want me to leave, I'm gone."

"No, no, stay stay stay," Jack said. "We'll smoke."

"I never thought anybody would take me seriously as a chaperon for God's sake." Karen lowered herself into a beanbag chair. "They never asked me to watch over any of Jen's school dances, that's for sure. I always loved this dome. Amazing that it's lasted so well."

Jack swept his eyes from floor to zenith. "Triangles make it strong."

"Aha," Jen exclaimed, wondering whether Jack had intended a pun, and wishing him to know that she had heard one.

"Do I remember that pipe from olden days?" Karen asked.

"You might," Jack said. "My pride and joy. Here is its case, and here's the special compartment for my stash, and opening it, we find the stash itself, some of which I shall insert into the cob for present sacrifice."

"You sound like a priest," Karen said.

They smoked.

"You got Country Joe and the Fish?" Karen asked, pointing to the iPod.

"No," Jack said. "I've got the Airplane, though, and Joni Mitchell, and the White Album."

"Christ, let's hear the White Album," Karen said. As Paul McCartney began to sing "Blackbird," she closed her eyes and subsided into her chair.

"Do you think it's snowing yet?" Jack asked Jen.

Looking up through the clouded plexiglas, Jen said, "Hard to say."

"If we listen maybe we'll hear the first flake hit the dome." Jack re-filled the pipe and they smoked again.

"I am really stoned," Jen said.

"Good thing your mother's here."

His *triangle* double entendre reminded Jack of his jealousy of Annie's thesis advisor, Professor Copernicus Ratner, whom Annie had referred to as PCR, or just CR.

"I'm meeting CR today," she had once announced, during their stay at the farm.

"You met him last week."

"Yes and now it's this week."

"Why doesn't he come out here?"

"Professors don't make house calls."

When they had that conversation, they were in bed together in their room in the farmhouse. Jack had begun to plan the dome. He was trying to master the geometry of domes. "How many sides to a dodecahedron?"

"Twenty," Annie had replied. She had an uncanny way of knowing things.

When she was gone Jack reached to the table on her side of the bed and picked up a book she had just acquired. It was *Our Bodies; Ourselves*. Its pictures distracted him from his jealousy. He had hated being jealous then and even now, in the dome with Jen and Karen, he disliked remembering how it had felt. Comparing his memory of earlier reactions to the present, he decided that the animal edge was gone; everything was easier now.

The door opened and Pamela stepped into the dome. "Hey guys."

"Lunchtime!" Karen said. To Jen she added, "Pizza, baby?" The two of them stood up and left.

Pamela looked at Jack. "Can I get some smoke?"

"Why not?"

As she sat down in the place Jen had vacated, Pamela said, "I guess everybody hates me and wishes I weren't here."

"I guess," Jack agreed. He softened and added, "I don't know, Pam—you are part of the history here. It's good that you came. Maybe you could have been a little quieter or should I say stone silent about Boomer last night. You know?"

"Yeah. Alcohol-induced poor judgment. I'll try to balance it out today with cannabis-induced poor judgment." She took a deep pull on the water pipe. Exhaling slowly, she said, "I don't know why sex is such a big deal anyway."

"It's how we're wired."

"Is sex a big deal to you?"

"Oh yeah."

"Still?"

"Oh yeah. I don't have the raring-to-go capacity I had when I was nineteen but I still think about it. More than I should. I don't suppose that's as true of women."

"I still love the attention." She watched Jack smoke. "If I was willing, would you want it from me?"

"I wouldn't want to hurt your feelings—but I think I could resist."

"How's that?"

"I don't seem to be in a libidinous frame of mind right now. That's one thing. And we would stand a good chance of getting caught, and I love Annie and don't want to have to explain how come I'm in your pants. Plus—how many men would you say you have slept with?"

"Just men? Not counting women?"

Jack just raised his eyebrows and looked at her.

"I lost count."

"Over a hundred though, right?"

"Way over a hundred. Does that matter?"

"Maybe it shouldn't but that kind of past has always been a turn-off to me."

"You only sleep with virgins."

"There aren't any. But believing that your partner has a certain selectivity is nice. There's kind of a partial chastity when making love at least means something about a relationship."

"Tell guys that. Meanwhile, if I were younger you might have a different response right now."

"Maybe." Jack looked vacant.

"What are you thinking about?"

"I admit I am obsessed with the bodies of beautiful women. Maybe you are, too?"

Pamela didn't say anything.

"Breasts. They should be as comic as their name of boobs. But no, they fascinate. Their curves, their colors, their promise."

"In the old days, you were cute."

Jack looked puzzled.

"You've put on some weight."

"I like food," Jack said. "And I think it's time for lunch."

As they walked to the house, it seemed too warm for snow. But an hour later, when the group returned from Greylock, a few scattered flakes were falling, and as everyone gathered in the kitchen to drink tea and eat goat cheese and crackers it began to snow in earnest. Cancellations for the party came by phone—the Vermonter's were staying home and so were the Northamptonites. At four-thirty Paul called and told his father he wasn't coming. He had been the last prospective guest. The caterer dropped off what was now way too much food. Because there was concern about returning to their lodgings before the roads became too bad, they decided to go ahead with the slide show. Jeff set up the screen and projector in the living room. Tea mugs were rinsed and filled with wine, bourbon, or seltzer. Jeff sounded his gong.

Annie looked around the room. The only couple sitting together was Elaine and Pam, who were holding hands. Duane was on the sofa between Jen and her mother. "Thanks, everybody, for sending me photos," Annie said. "It was fun to scan them and to see how they fit together." After a few pictures of the first weeks at the farm, Annie showed one of Duane with a paintbrush. "It looks like he got more paint on his shirt than on the house."

"At nineteen I was a klutz. You guys took in a child."

"For anyone who doesn't recognize them," Annie said, "this is Carol and Karen in the kitchen."

"Carol!" Karen said. "Check out her hair."

"There I am in my overalls with the hammer loop! And I've got my hammer," Elaine said. "Ready for anything. I still have that hammer."

"She used it on me this morning," Bob said.

The slide changed. "There's Boomer and his Harley," Karen said. "His hog, he called it. We rode many a mile on that thing."

There were a few pictures of the septic system being installed. Then came 1974.

"Look at all the garden seeds Duane started."

"Yeah but I didn't know what I was doing. I started them too early. And I wasn't good at transplanting.

"We had a great garden though."

"That's because Hoeth came in May and we started all over."

"Annie and I moved in a month after her," Jack said.

When the slides reached the point of Annie and Jack's arrival, the photography improved. When Annie showed her pictures of fencing the pasture, Duane said, a little louder than was necessary, "I wish Hoeth were here; she would have loved these."

Annie tried to figure out what that meant. Was he proclaiming loyalty to his wife? As she continued her narration, Annie looked around the room. Elaine seemed subdued. Making up with Pamela, or the opportunity to lecture Bob, or both, had calmed her.

Outdoors the silent snow fell faster than anyone realized.

"Jack and I got here early that summer," Annie said. "Here's the barn from the side where the dome will be. Pre-dome."

"I was reading my Bucky Fuller, my Edward Popko," Jack said. "Making my plans."

"There I am again," Pamela said. "Without Bob—he was off meeting the love of his life."

"Yes I met her but she was still going with another guy," Bob said. At that time he had still considered himself Pamela's boyfriend— while she had been sleeping with others—including Boomer. Aware of those associations, more sensitive to them now than when she had made the slide show, Annie didn't leave that picture on the screen for long. Pumpkins dominated the next slide.

"Value those pumpkins! Hoeth and I grew them," Duane said. "We had so many! They were a sign of how great the Halloween party was going to be. These are Annie's pictures, right? Beautifully composed. I've never seen them."

"Neither have I," Jack said.

"Nobody has," Annie said. I never printed them. I just made contact sheets and put them away until now. I scanned the negatives."

A slender Jack presided proudly at the grand opening of his dome—Jeff and Philip both held scissors ready to cut the ribbon across the door—a hippie send-up of the straight-world big-wigs showing off their status. There were people in costumes, playing games. "Isn't that—" Ruth started to ask Bob, but the slide changed quickly. Fuzzy low-contrast images of the group doing Murder in the

Dark were followed by brighter shots, taken the next morning, of the Halloween party's aftermath.

Annie said "I also have McBrew's movie of the party. I'll show it after the stills."

"Paul!" Elaine said, responding to a picture of her, from the side, in her last month of her pregnancy, followed by pictures of the childbirth in the kitchen. Pamela was in the corner trying to look like a shaman. Philip was on the telephone—"Checking with Doctor Dad," Elaine said. There was the midwife holding wet little Paul.

The next picture showed Barb and Jeff together in a photo booth. Barb had not been long at North Road—the bond with Jeff had come quickly. They were already a comfortable couple in this strip of three pictures, calm and close. Barb had told Annie that this strip of paper was her most precious possession. The affection between Jeff and Barb seemed so effortless. Annie felt wrong about having taken Duane's hand only a few hours before. She didn't look at Jack with her eyes— but inwardly she saw his face—droll, tolerant, intelligent. She felt lucky to have him.

The next pictures were a series Annie had taken of the memorial Karen had improvised on the roadside where Boomer had crashed. She said, "Karen made this. For Boomer. Remember? She did it the day after he died on Route 20. Jack later proved that you can follow that highway all the way to the Pacific. Boomer, on his bike in bad weather, stopped here, as we all remember; his death was the worst thing that could have happened to us as a group—because as Philip has pointed out, we could never figure out how to respond to Boomer. Not really."

"We failed him and we failed Karen and Jen, too," Phil said, "but I don't beat us up because we were still kids and still working the problem and then this happened and prevented us from succeeding. We were stuck."

"A few months later Karen left to have Jen," Annie said, "and Hoeth and Duane moved to Minnesota and I got a job in Maine and by the end of Seventy-five we were all gone except for Barb and Jeff."

The only sound in the room was Karen sobbing. The mounting snow, which muffled all outdoors, seemed to have quieted everything everywhere. The closing sequence of slides showed the farmhouse, the barn, the chickens, the garden, and finally a group picture. "Here we are," Annie said, "Close friends, yet strangers to each other."

"No," Duane said, "Not strangers."

"Okay" Annie agreed. "Or we are and we aren't. We don't want to be. When we ask each other questions, sometimes we don't understand what the other wants to know. First you're a kid by yourself and then you pick up some friends and allies but still, in the end—"

"In the end there's still the love," Jack said.

"Yes," Phil said.

"I wish I felt that," Elaine said.

"I wish you did too," Phil said.

"I know we really do care about each other," Annie said. We want to feel close—but we're all so different. Anyway, to end on an upbeat note I'll show the movie McBrew shot at the Halloween party."

"That was our high-water point," Phil said. "Joy-wise."

"Not for me," Jeff said. "Barb wasn't here yet."

The film had been taken outdoors, in daylight. It showed young people carving pumpkins. Then the same people playing volleyball. Duane, big and energetic, dominated the court.

"Where were you?" Barb asked Jeff.

"Off somewhere," Jeff said.

The last minute of the film was in dim blue light. People in costumes were lighting candles in jack-o-lanterns. A pickup truck pulled into the background and a man in a wolf mask got out of the cab.

"There's Jeff," Annie said. The screen went white, then black, and she added, "The End." Everyone applauded.

The first person to say goodnight and head for his car was Duane—but he was soon back indoors. "I don't think anybody's going anywhere," he announced. "We're snowed in."

Jeff left to reconnoiter.

"Pajama party!" Pam shouted.

"There aren't enough beds," Karen said.

"We can manage." Barb explained that because each summer their nieces and nephews had visited for what they all called "Farm Camp" they had plenty of inflatable mattresses.

Jeff returned. "It's been coming down really fast," he reported. "We could dig out the cars and I could clear the driveway, but North Road isn't plowed. I called the town—they won't get here until morning. So, sorry, you're stuck here."

Ruth and Bob went to the room that had been assigned to them. They didn't have luggage to unpack but they went in, anyway, to take possession. When the door was closed Ruth asked, "Did you enjoy yourself at that party?"

"What party?"

"The Halloween party we just saw the movie of."

"What makes you think I was there?"

"I remember that shirt you had when we were first going out. I thought I recognized the pattern in the black and white picture and then in the movie the color looked just like it."

"Well, you're right, it was me. Jeff and I had worn the same masks the year before at the farm—we had been the wolf twins. So that next year we wore the same masks, but he went to my party and I went to his."

"Why did you do that?"

"Churchez la femme. He was single and still sad over losing Carol. He was on the prowl. I wanted to surprise Pam—who turned out not to be here."

"Where was she?"

"She had left with Elaine, who was mad at everybody over something. She had stomped off, and Pam went to keep her company.

198

By the time I knew Pam was gone, the others had taken me for Jeff. I kept my mouth shut and went with it. Just for fun."

When they went downstairs, Ruth found Barb. "That wolf in the movie? Who arrived in Jeff's truck? That was Bob."

"Bob?"

"Yes. I recognized his shirt and he admitted that he and Jeff had swapped Halloween parties."

At supper during a pause in conversation Barb said, "Ruth told me a funny thing about the movie Annie showed. We all thought that was Jeff in the wolf mask. But it wasn't."

Annie's head jerked up. "Who was it?"

"It was Bob," Ruth said.

Bob kept his eyes in the middle of the table, apparently studying the centerpiece. "I apologize to anyone who feels misled," he said. "It was kind of a stupid kid thing to have done."

Annie looked at Karen.

Incredulous, Karen looked at Bob. "It was you?"

Bob made a face of regretful acknowledgment.

Karen blushed.

Pamela said, "Uh oh. I get it."

Karen left the table.

Annie whispered in Bob's ear, "I have to talk to you."

When Jen went upstairs to check on her mother, she found her seated on the edge of the bed. "What's the matter?" Jen asked.

"Honey, I have something important to tell you."

Jen sat down next to her mother. "Okay."

"It's complicated. I kind of should have told you a long time ago but there were good reasons why I didn't."

"Okay."

"I have never really been sure that Boomer Justice was your father, because we didn't, we hadn't, I don't think . . ."

"Who did you think it was?"

"Until tonight I thought it was Jeff because of something that happened at that Halloween party but I never told because I had a thing for him but he went for Barb as though I didn't exist and when Boomer died I realized everyone would assume that he was your dad and I just would keep you for myself."

"Mom."

Karen began to cry. "And I never knew you would care so much about the dad thing—I should have known—but Jeff and Barb were always sweet to you so I thought everything was okay."

They were both crying. Karen had one arm around Jen's shoulder.

"So I just never said anything because, you know, we'd both had a few drinks, it was an accident we'd hid in the same closet during the game—I thought he was Jeff—I always wished Jeff had loved me—"

"Oh oh oh."

"And now it turns out it was his brother." Karen put her other arm around her daughter and said, wetly, into her ear, "Honey, I'm so, so, sorry. I messed up but I love you."

After a short conversation with Annie, Bob took Ruth to their room. "I didn't know you were going to out me about this."

"What's the big deal?"

"Because of what happened. During that game of Murder in the Dark, when all the lights are out, I hid in a closet. Someone else had the same idea. We were both drunk and close together, you know, and got turned on. At first I didn't know who it was—I was imagining this girl from Vermont, but eventually I realized it was Karen."

"Did you have intercourse?"

"I think so. We might have. I'm not sure. Maybe. I guess we did. Because Annie just told me that Karen told her that Jen is—Jen was—that I might be—we'll have to find out."

"Oh Christ Bob."

Annie said, "Do you know what this means?"

Jack looked puzzled. "What?"

"That Bob and Jeff traded places?"

"No."

"It means that our friend Bob fathered of our friend Jen."

"What?"

"Karen thought that the guy in the closet was Jeff and didn't want to say anything."

"Boomer was her father," Jack said.

"Karen doesn't think so."

"What's Bob got to do with it?"

"I just told you—she thought she did it with Jeff in the dark, but now it turns out it was Bob."

"Why didn't he say anything?"

"You can ask him."

After Jeff and Barb took apart the temporary table and restored the living room to its usual appearance, they sat down on the sofa. "Do you understand what the hell is going on?" Jeff asked.

"Did you switch places with your brother like they said?"

"Yeah. Just for the hell of it. He wanted to see Pam and I thought maybe I'd meet somebody at his party."

"Why did you keep it a secret?"

"He'd whiffed on Pam—she wasn't there—and he thought he would look pathetic to everyone, chasing around after her, and because he'd driven back to Boston in the middle of the night—which he never should have done—and everybody at the farm was sound asleep when I showed up in the morning. They just thought I was coming back from town with muffins from the bakery—nobody ever said anything."

"And did you meet somebody?"

"No and not long after I met you. Why has this become a big deal all of a sudden—because it was a secret?"

"No, because—"

Barb stopped as Ruth and Bob came out of their bedroom. Bob said, "Do you know where Jen and Karen are?"

Barb pointed up. "Karen's in the room at the back."

Bob led Ruth up the stairs. The door was closed. Bob knocked softly.

"Who is it?" Karen's voice came through the door.

"Bob and Ruth."

Silence.

"May we come in?"

"All right," Karen said. She and Jen were on the bed.

Ruth closed the door.

Bob looked at Jen. "I don't know what's for sure or what might turn out to be or not to be—but I guess you know people are saying we might be related."

Without looking up, Jen nodded. Tears ran down her face.

"If it's true I just want you to know how sorry I am that I haven't done my part all these years."

"That's my fault," Karen said. "In a way."

Bob continued to address Jen. "You have a great mom. Although we don't know each other very well you seem wonderful to me. I know that Barb and my brother love you."

"We want you to know," Ruth said, "that if love from us is acceptable to you, we have it to offer. No matter how the biological stuff turns out."

Karen stood up and embraced Ruth.

Jen looked at Bob. "Mom says you're my dad but she thought it was Jeff."

"That's what I'm hearing, too," Bob said. "It doesn't reflect well on me."

Jen put her hands over her face. Karen tugged Jen to her feet and hugged her.

Bob and Ruth stood by awkwardly until Karen, keeping one arm around Jen, took Ruth's hand in her other hand and said, "I can't believe this is happening," and laughed. "I really can't." They all laughed. They stood there, wiping their eyes, crying and laughing.

Several hours later, Duane found Phil at the kitchen table. Philip looked up and said, "I brought some old Scotch in case of emergencies. Tonight qualifies. Want some?"

Duane sat down. "You are a gentleman."

"You acquiesce." As Phil poured, he asked, "What's next for you? I heard you might not go home."

"You get good information. What now? Who knows? At the moment I'm wishing Annie didn't have as good a marriage as she seems to have."

"That thought has occurred to me off and on over the years."

"Tonight you and I are the woman-less men."

"I am accustomed to being so. Unlike you."

"Is your life as solitary as it seems?"

"No. I am thoroughly en-meshed. Socially."

"I've wondered if you were gay."

"Probably lots of people assume that I am. My gay friends know otherwise."

Duane said, "Could I ask you something?"

"Go ahead."

"The atmosphere changed around here after supper. Do you know what is going on?"

"Yes. Annie's slide show inadvertently demonstrated that Boomer was not the biological father of Karen's wonderful daughter."

"Has someone else stepped forward?"

"Mr. Robert Quarless fails to deny that he is possibly, probably, or assuredly responsible."

"Ah." Duane considered. "Is everyone pissed at him?"

"I was, but I'm over it."

"Why? He could count to nine months, couldn't he?"

"An hour ago he sat where you are and gave me his point of view."

"What was that?"

"He wasn't tuned in to what happened with Karen, and he had other concerns, which reminded me how true that was for all of us. Shall I sketch the sequence and situation?"

"By all means."

"An intoxicated graduate student has an unexpected casual erotic encounter which might or might not have involved actual penetration. Back in his real life he meets his bride-to-be and focuses on her and school. By the time, weeks later, that Karen thinks she's pregnant, Boomer is dead. Karen is doubly bereft, because Barb has arrived and Jeff fell for her right away. Convinced that she's carrying Jeff's child, Karen leaves the farm, goes home to Worcester, and drops out of touch. We at the farm eventually learn that she had a baby and we all assume it's Boomer's. Jeff probably never mentioned the birth to his brother. He's not sure that he even mentioned her pregnancy. As far as Bob can remember it was years before he learned that Karen had a child."

"And he was too busy getting ready to make money in computers to pay much attention."

"A harsh way to frame it, but not without truth," Phil said.

Duane looked out the window. "Are you disappointed that the reunion got snowed out?"

"It didn't. We had it. It was only the outsiders who were kept away. It's too bad that Paul couldn't make it—but the North Road farmers, the real ones, were all here."

"There was conflict."

"Conflict does not shock me. Did it cause your wife's departure?"

"No. That's about us. We'd grown apart, as they say."

It was still dark when Jeff came into the kitchen. "It's stopped snowing. I'm going to dig us out."

Phil offered to help. The three men shoveled out the cars. By sunrise, the road was open. The autumn snow, warmed from above and below, soon collapsed. In a few days everyone was gone, and the goats were back in their pasture.

We understand then do we not?
What I promis'd without mentioning it, have you not accepted?
What the study could not teach—what the preaching could not
accomplish is accomplish'd, is it not?
–Walt Whitman

14

On Sundays during football season, Phil and Paul had a routine. Phil took a pizza to his son's apartment—an upstairs of a duplex in suburban Boston—and they watched whatever games were being broadcast.

Paul greeted his father with, "What did you get?"

"For pizza? Moose-meat and mushroom," Phil replied. "Hello Paul."

"Moose not venison? Not beaver-tail?"

"They claimed it was sausage but it smells like moose to me."

"You've never smelled moose."

"Have you?"

"Sure. Nate stews it at Northeast Carry. Serves it to any guest who wants it."

"Northeast Carry. Where is that?"

"The northeast corner of Moosehead Lake."

"What get's carried?"

"Your canoe. Your traps. Northeast Carry is the shortest portage from the lake to the Penobscot River. You jump from one Maine watershed to the next. And if you want to go even farther north you paddle to another portage and hop over to the Allagash."

"Great names. All those syllables. I invited Duane to join us."

"Who?"

"Duane. He's a North Road Farm guy who came to the party and seems to be sticking around.

"How was the reunion?"

"Oh, man." Phil slumped into the couch. "It was lively. It had consequences."

Paul handed his father a beer. "A major Boomer-fest."

That confused Phil. Why would his son be mentioning the long-lost motorcycle hippie? Then he realized that Paul referred to the generation of the North Road Farmers. "Yes. Yes. A counter-culture rally."

"Lots of admiration for how cool you were. How advanced in your thinking."

"A little of that. Not too much."

"Elaine says we're going backwards," Paul said. His mother had never allowed him to call her *Mom* so he referred to his parents as Elaine and Dad. New acquaintances assumed that Elaine was his step-mother.

"She makes her case strongly," Phil said.

"Indeed." Her son and her ex-husband, better than anyone, knew the force of Elaine's opinions.

After a few minutes watching the game, Phil said, "Last weekend's event was not so much about our generation. It more just about a few human-beings stumbling through their lives."

"The human species—your specialty."

"Yes. I was like a bird-lover in a tropical forest. So much to observe. The big news though was about your friend Jen."

"Oh. Does she have a new guy?"

"You haven't heard?"

"Heard what?"

"She changed fathers."

"What?"

"Turns out that Karen never truly thought that Boomer was the paternal contributor, as it were."

Paul looked at his father with slack-jawed surprise.

"She thought Jeff had done the deed but because he behaved coldly about their intimate moment—that was her perception at the time—she let everyone think it was Boomer. Including Jen. I'm surprised Jen hasn't filled you in on this."

"I haven't talked to her."

"She seemed to take it calmly enough. All considered."

"Her father is Jeff?"

"No—not Jeff. His brother Bob."

"Jeff's brother?"

"Yes. You might not know him."

"Too weird."

Looking back at the television, Phil asked, "Do you care who wins?"

"Not really."

"What have you been up to?"

"Work. I can't believe this about Jen."

"You should call her."

"She's mad because I didn't drive out to Dutton."

"So you have talked to her."

"No. I talked to her when she was there. Before the snow. She wanted me to come."

"Ah."

"And I was going to—but then the snow."

"Right."

"She doesn't want to date me but she complained I left her alone with you senior citizens so basically I can't win."

"Complicated."

"How did this revelation come about?"

Phil explained, adding, "I guess it's not for sure yet. They are going to do tests and all. It's unclear what happened in that closet—fumbling impulsive heat, in costumes, both high, neither sure who they were with. In those days, such things happened."

"You think they've stopped?"

"Young people seem a little saner now."

"Huh."

"More responsible. On the whole."

"Far out."

"What?"

"Isn't that what you guys used to say? Back in the day?"

"Far out?"

"Yeah."

"What is?"

"Jen! Changing fathers."

The doorbell rang. When Duane stepped into the room Phil had the sensation of an odd displacement—his son matched the way he remembered Duane—burly and bearded, whereas Duane was clean shaven, and slender, which, combined with a certain physical restraint, gave him an air of delicacy.

"Did your dad tell you why I wanted to talk with you?" Duane asked Paul.

"No. I didn't realize that you did want to talk with me."

"I do, because I heard that you guide outdoor trips."

"True."

"Among my kids are two who have agreed in principle to go camping with me next summer. None of us have great outdoor skills but we don't want to do the recreational vehicle campground type thing—we want some kind of real camping, in a wild place. We need help and I'm told you are a guy who could be of assistance."

For the next hour Phil watched his son communicate information and enthusiasm, gather information, and make recommendations.

"Do I have it right?" Paul asked Duane. "Two married couples, two granddaughters, one grandson—he would be the youngest at five."

"That's right."

"Backpacking—not for your group," Paul said. "Not with such young kids. Canoe camping could work, though, if you are up for that."

Duane thought that sounded good and wanted to hear more about it.

Paul described the campsites maintained by Maine and the state's clean, clear waters. "Lobster Lake," Paul said. "I could take you there."

"Lobster Lake," Duane echoed. The sound of the place rested in the room. "Lobster Lake. Let's go to Lobster Lake."

When the game ended and the two older men had left, Paul texted Jen. *I hear you had an eventful weekend.*

Like hands, ideas and beliefs are instruments for coping.
–John Dewey paraphrased by Louis Menand

15

"I read some of your stuff," Vogelsong said.

"Ah," Phil said.

"You call one of your pieces 'The Taxonomy of Love.' You received a lot of recognition for that."

"Gratifyingly true."

"Parts of it are useful. But what you said about polyamory—will you admit that's mere justification for doing whatever you want?"

"When people react that way, they wishfully imagine an all-fulfilling relationship with their spouses—or they deny a disappointment they can't admit."

"What brings you back to me so many months after our initial meeting?"

"I thought you should hear the other shoe hit the floor."

"My notes remind me that you were vague about what you wished to accomplish."

"You, on the other hand, were clear that watching me wander across my existential desert was not worth your time."

"Right."

"When I was here before, people were planning the fortieth anniversary of my group house."

"Did it go well?"

"No. And yes. It was snowed out, partly. And my son never made it. But the core group was there. I fell for Annie all over again, but she only has eyes for a tall Westerner, and also for her husband, but not for me although we have become collaborators, sort of, in her photo project.

"The party had a reveal. The woman who was conceived during my years at the farm was the fruit of a different paternal parent than anyone had supposed. On the one hand, no one much likes such surprises so far downstream in life; on the other hand the woman wished she had a father and now it appears that the man welcomes the advent of a daughter. So maybe it's all good; time will tell, especially if it turns out that getting a dad makes the lady more available to my son.

"As for him, God I love him so, and what else can I say, really? He never made it to Dutton—he dithered, then came the snow—you see that everything went wrong—snow in October—it trapped the inner circle—my ex-wife fighting with her girlfriend; Annie's slide show revealing photographic evidence of past sins, like in that Antonioni movie we all loved; while we're stuck in the house—persons in a snow-globe. And me, trying to flirt with Annie but she fascinated with Duane—only Lydia's love keeps me from feeling pathetic and clownish. The group acknowledged my role in the old days, the days of our most intense becoming. That felt good. Since then we seem to have delegated all becoming to our kids, while we ourselves just aged. Paul tells me that young ravens seek novelty but older ravens fear it. Me, though, I still look for the new and different—new clients with new stories, new girlfriends with new tastes and turns of mind, new places, shops, cuisines.

"Anyway, I sent Annie the nuggets of prose and poetry that I had found in my readings. I had left them in knotholes. Hollow trees. My naturalist son says they would be have been studied by flying squirrels and screech owls. Annie, everyone's ideal lady, interviewed me into remembering that weird habit. Afterward I looked in my files and I found the carbons I had made when I typed them. I sent them to her. She decided to combine them with pictures—she's a photographer—and now she is exhibiting the combination in a coffee shop. So, cool, and the reunion led to that."

"Do you still like the ideas?"

"Yes. But in the intervening decades I've come to my own take on life, on being a person."

"You reached your intellectual destination?"

"Maybe. Clients come to me wanting healing. I respond with a teaching. Some people seem to benefit."

"And your instruction is?"

"Not original. Grandmothers know it. I tell people, use your interpersonal loom to weave. Make a fabric that supports those you care for, that saves them, in that old usage, from falling. Create the warp and woof of relationships, a supporting loving web, the many colors of the good stuff I call care-love. We lay down that rainbow silk of care-love strand after strand and bind it to the cloth of our dear ones.

"What secures the corners? The mass of nurturing up through the generations—we anchor to that. The people who spun your care-love tied into their mother's, their grandfather's, their poet's, their companion's.

"Jeff, my long-time best friend—he and I both had decent parents and then he found Sam and Rebecca, the old lady and the old man next door. You could see the difference in Jeff when he came back from their place—he was calmer. It jumped out at me because I had married a lady whose childhood had lacked quality care-love, and she tended to create tension.

"Anyway, my counsel has always been: inner peace comes from relatedness. Each, according to our fortune, has inherited family—but whether that legacy is thick or thin you must also tie off elsewhere— to the care of peers, to nature, to the arts. In my case I will name Walt Whitman who offered himself in precisely this sense. Tolstoy and Shakespeare also link me to the universe. Others would cleave to music, as the blues for Skeets, Janis Joplin for Karen, or to nature, where Thoreau placed his bets, and so does my son.

"In marriage we hope to find the number one reciprocator of care-love and the opportunity to nurture children and grandchildren—sweet, unconditional closeness. So I teach people to spin fibers of care and weave them into fruitful relationships. The work is done by talk that encourages, liberates, and appreciates. What safety we can ever have, as mortal beings, we have through our ties to others."

"Okay. That stuff works for you I guess," Vogelsong said.

"Not for you?"

"Relationships are what they are. Complicated. But, what we call peace of mind, really, is all just brain chemistry."

"Right."

"Right."

The sum of all known reverence I add up in you, whoever you
are.

–Walt Whitman

16

Standing in water over her ankles, bending over her canoe, Jen hoped Paul wouldn't offer advice, or, worse yet, start repositioning gear. He did not—he stayed busy supervising the loading of the other three boats. When he was finished, he asked Jen to make sure everything got tied in.

"While you're gone?"

"Yes."

"In all the canoes?"

"Yes."

"When do you think you'll be back?"

"It will be at least an hour each way."

Paul and Jen were guiding Duane's family river trip in the north woods of Maine. Three of the four automobiles were about to be driven to the end-point, at the far end of a big lake called Chesuncook. Two cars would be left there; the drivers would return in the third. The distance was not huge, but the route lay round-about over unpaved logging roads.

After the vehicles left Jen worked for half an hour to make sure that all the gear was lashed to the canoes. When the last dry-bag had been bound to a thwart with nylon cord, Jen stood up straight and listened. It was quiet. She could hear water shushing over the low dam just upstream. She heard a raven's *kuk* in the middle distance. Noticing the absence of human speech, Jen turned toward the bank, where a woman sat reading a book, and said, "You're Brit, right?"

"Right! I don't know how you are going to keep us all straight. I'm Brit and my sister-in-law who drove away is Beth."

"And Beth, if I remember correctly, is Duane's daughter and you are married to his son Tom."

"Yes and we have the two girls. Sylvan and Charlotte. Whereas Beth and Troy have the little boy. Teddie."

Jen noted the rhyme between the dad's name and the word "boy"—she habitually looked for mnemonics. "Where are the others?"

"The dads took the kids for a hike. The cars will be gone quite a while, right?"

"True."

"I felt like I should have been helping you but I didn't know what to do and you looked like you had it under control. Aren't your feet freezing? Isn't the water cold?"

"It is and they are but they'll warm up." Jen told the woman that the next job was to make lunch and suggested that they could work together on that.

"I'm happy to help," Brit said, "but why don't we just let everyone make their own?"

"Two reasons. First, that can result in unfair division of available provisions. Second, we want to leave as soon as the vehicles return so we can find a campsite and still have daylight for pitching tents and cooking."

As Jen produced sandwich-making materials Brit said, "It seems kind of stereotyped to have the moms making sandwiches. But I guess since the men have the kids I can stand it."

Jen twisted hard to open a jar of peanut butter.

"I said moms but I should have said women. Or are you a mom?"

"No—no kids, no husband, just me."

"But you and Paul are sort of a couple, right?"

"No, but people tend to think that. I guess because we've known each other a long time and we've been guiding together."

"My father-in-law says he lived with both of your mothers at a commune?"

"That's right. Last fall was its fortieth anniversary party. A reunion you might say. That's the first time I met Duane and Hoeth."

"Oh my god—you know my mother-in-law?"

Jen made a face that, she hoped, communicated a sympathetic surmise about having Hoeth as your mother-in-law.

"The first time Tom took me home to the farm—that was very nearly the last time, also."

"Yikes."

"Oh my god."

"I can imagine. But you married Tom anyway."

"Yes. Granddaddy Duane saved us."

"Are they permanently split now?"

"I suppose—I don't know. He's gone back two or three times but I think that was just to formalize the arrangement and get some stuff. He seems to be settling into his new place."

The voices of the returning hikers broke into the conversation. When the families—the two young couples and their three children—were together, their exclusive focus on each other made Jen feel invisible. She would have been resentful if she had been there as a friend—but as a guide, being an invisible functionary was expected and often preferred.

Lunch was gobbled down; Jen had her daily humus-and-jelly-on-whole-wheat sandwich. When the drivers returned they were each handed lunches in plastic bags. The cars were locked. As soon as everyone was wearing a flotation vest, the heavily-laden canoes were pushed out to the edge of navigable water. Adults held the canoes while the children stepped aboard. When they were settled, the bow paddlers took their places. Standing in shallow water, the stern paddlers pointed the boats toward the middle of the river. Jen lifted one foot and placed it in front of her seat, on the canoe's center line, leaned down to grip one gunwale in each hand, and called "Ready?"

From the bow Duane nodded and replied, "Ready." His grandson, seated behind him on the floor of the canoe, was wide-eyed and silent.

With the foot that was still under water, Jen gave a short kick at the gravel, shifted her weight over the canoe, and sensed acceleration as the current took the boat. After one quick water-shedding shake, Jen pulled her trailing foot aboard, lowered herself to her seat, lifted her paddle, and steered the little craft into line with the others. By proceeding in single file the first canoe could demonstrate it was on a navigable course through shallow places, or, if it ran aground, could suggest that the other boats try a different route. This river had been chosen for the family adventure because it lacked white-water. The speed of the current and the depth of the water varied as they went along, but at no point did they have to negotiate boulder-strewn rapids. In late summer, the West Branch of the Penobscot offered easy boating.

A minute after Jen's canoe was launched, the little passenger asked a question. "Where are we going to sleep?"

"At Lobster Lake," Jen replied.

"In the lake?"

"No," Jen said. "At a campsite on shore. A nice campsite, I hope. First come first serve."

In the bow, Duane glanced over his shoulder. "Why is the lake called Lobster?"

"I'm not sure. Some say it's because the loggers found lots of crayfish there," Jen answered. "Others say it's because it's shaped like a lobster claw, with one big lobe and one small one. That's probably it, but I don't think anyone knows."

"Are there bears at Lobster Lake?" asked the little boy.

"Bears do live around here," Jen said. "But they never bother people. They are afraid of us."

The boy lifted his arms above his head, curled his fingers toward his grandfather's back, and roared a quiet roar.

"Are you a bear?" Jen asked.

"No," Teddie said. "I scare bears."

"He's a person who scares bears," Teddie's mother said, in a stage whisper, to her husband. Their canoe had slowed and fallen into position beside Jen and Duane's. Now it slowed even more and dropped behind. Teddie gave a quick glance over his shoulder at his mother, then looked forward. Jen thought he squared his little shoulders a bit as he faced the wild world without his parents in his field of view. When she thought about how Troy and Beth had floated by to make their proximity known to the little boy, Jen realized that she had witnessed a bit of parenting.

The blue sky turned gray. A light rain began to fall. As soon as everyone had donned a rain coat or poncho, the clouds broke up and the sun came back. Jen saw Paul turn the lead canoe and disappear to the right; he had entered Lobster Stream. When her own canoe made the turn, Jen exclaimed, "Otters!" Two silver-black streaks disappeared into the water of the stream. A few minutes later, entering Lobster Lake, they were greeted by a wild call.

"What's that?" Teddie asked.

"It's a loon," Duane answered. "Isn't that a great sound?"

"What's a loon?"

"It's a bird," explained his grandfather. "It looks a little like a duck. Maybe we'll see it. They have pointed beaks."

Paddling across the still deep water of the lake on the windless afternoon, Jen relaxed. Why did she feel so good? The physical activity in a wild outdoor place. The focus on the others—paying customers inexperienced at camping. The wide-eyed child seated between her and his grandfather gave her pleasure. She wondered what her half-brother would have been like at that age. How would she have regarded him, as his older sister? For the thousandth time she marveled that she had an actual father—and a whole new set of relatives.

The canoes landed on the beach at their campsite—a peninsula in the big lake. Everyone helped empty the boats and lug the gear up the bank to the picnic tables. Tom and Troy found the dry bag that contained the tents and started setting them up. Paul put a tarp over the picnic tables—rain threatened again, but once the tents were up and the dining and cooking area under cover, rain would cause no difficulty. Charlotte and her mother headed into the woods to find the privy—leaving Sylvan with Jen. Jen asked, "Have you done a lot of camping?"

"Some," Sylvan replied. Behind her, not far out onto the lake, a loon laughed loudly.

"I love that sound," Jen said.

"It is amazing."

"I love your name, too," Jen added.

"I hate it."

"Why?"

"Because people always call me Silly."

"Oh. Too bad."

"It's my weird parent's fault. Sylvan has to do with trees I guess."

"And here you are exploring the Great North Woods of Maine. Plenty of trees here. Not much other than trees, except lakes and a few moose and eagles and osprey."

"It's so quiet here. Aren't you married?"

"No. Maybe someday—maybe not."

"I wonder what I'll end up wanting," the girl said.

"You mean like whether you'll hope for a husband and a family?"

"Right."

"You have plenty of time to decide."

Holding up the tent poles, the girl asked, "How do these go?"

Jen showed her the sleeves in the tent that held the poles, and the reinforced fabric cups that held the ends of the poles when they were flexed. Suddenly the limp thin nylon, a formless pile, turned into an igloo-shaped shelter.

"Somebody did a lot of planning," the girl said, "to make this fit together."

"You're right," Jen said. "I never thought about it that way."

The fabric, poles, the planned-for tension, had become a sturdy lightweight wigwam in the campsite—a refuge from insects,—but, because it was roofed with mosquito netting, not from rain. Jen held up the outer cover of nylon. "I never can decide when to put on the rain fly,"

"The what?"

"Rain fly. That's what they call this last layer. It's waterproof."

"Oh."

"It goes over everything else and keeps out rain and wind and gives you privacy."

"Why don't they just make that the tent to begin with?"

"It would be like sleeping in a plastic bag."

"Oh."

"Not too healthy. The way this works, air gets in under the edge of the rain fly and through the netting so you can breathe and also so moisture can get out."

"Why does moisture need to get out? I mean, how would it get in?"

"From our bodies. From our breath. Shall we put our stuff in?"

"Okay." The loon called again. "Why is it making that sound?"

"I don't know," Jen said. "They just do that. I suppose it tells other loons 'I am here' but I don't know why that does them any good. Maybe it keeps competition away from their fishing."

"Fishing?"

"They eat fish."

"How do you know all this stuff?"

"I've been here before. People tell you things. You watch. You read. Over time you learn stuff."

After supper, the group gathered around the fire—but the girls were soon sleepy, and Jen was tired, too, so the three of them went to their tent. Charlotte curled up in her sleeping bag and closed her eyes. Sylvan read a few pages with her headlamp, then she turned it off and fell asleep. Jen watched firelight flicker on the side of the tent, and heard men's voices from the campfire, and some laughter, and let rest overtake her.

She awakened in the dark, hearing steady rain falling on the tent. When Jen sat up, Sylvan said, "I have to go to the bathroom."

"Okay. Do you want to go right now or do you want to wait in case maybe the rain is going to let up a little?"

"I can wait a while."

Water poured onto the tent. The sound of it and the knowledge that the girl had to go, made Jen also feel the need. "Maybe we should go ahead."

"Okay."

"Can you find your raincoat?"

"I think so."

Their stir and their headlamps awakened Charlotte. "What's going on?"

"We're going to the bathroom. Want to go?"

"No. Yes."

In raincoats, shod with flip-flops, the three left the tent. Jen held Charlotte's hand in one of hers, and a plastic bag with toilet paper in the other. When her headlamp shone on the wood of the outhouse, Sylvan asked, "Can I go first?"

"Yes," Jen said.

She started forward, but, when her sister asked Jen, "Could you please check for spiders before my turn?" she froze in her tracks.

Water dripped from all three raincoats.

"Why don't I check right now?" Jen shone her headlamp onto all the interior surfaces she could see through the open door. Then she went inside to check the corners.

As the door closed, Sylvan confided to her younger sister. "I can't believe I'm doing this."

"It's so dark," Charlotte said.

Jen reappeared. "All clear."

Sylvan went in and closed the door.

To Jen, Charlotte whispered, "This is fun."

When they had returned to the comfort of their warm, dry, sleeping bags, Jen listened as the rhythm of the two girls' breathing slowed. She thought, *Maybe it would be nice to have kids.*

210123

www.ingramcontent.com/pod-product-compliance
Lightning Source LLC
Chambersburg PA
CBHW070451120726
47910CB00003B/999

* 9 7 8 0 9 9 8 3 6 1 9 7 0 *